BOONS

A NOVELLA BY

DAVID OHLE

ISBN-13: 978-0-9798080-8-1
ISBN-10: 0-9798080-8-1

This tale would not have been told without major contributions, including portions of text, from my friend, the Professor himself, H.R. Hepburn of Grahamstown, South Africa.

Art/design by Derek White.

Published by Calamari Press

www.calamaripress.com

BOONS

One midwinter, during his post-graduate years in West Africa, where he studied simian variants, the Professor needed brood. He was on the telephone discussing the matter with the regional dealer.

"I need some brood. I will pay whatall."

"Well, Professor, it is winter and I don't want the little ones to get brood chill."

"They won't. I will move fast. Can I have them or not?"

"Very well, go and get them. They are on the farm at Wonderboom. You must be careful because the road is *middelmannetjie*, as we say. Very bad. The ruts are deep, the middle high."

"*Ja, nee*. I'll use the truck."

"What truck?"

"The one at Medical School we use to fetch the boons from Frankenwald."

"How many do you have out there?"

"We have a quarantine and keep hundreds of them."

"For what? What do you use them for?"

"Every department goes through them like a dose of salts. My own department probably kills ten or more a week."

"Why do they kill them?"

"I don't suppose they mean to, necessarily, but that is how the experiments go. Largely unsuccessful I would say. These are early strains. No good, really. I'm waiting until they get much better before I get myself one."

"What do you do with the dead ones?"

"You know that smell in Hillbrow on Thursdays?"

"I keep the windows closed."

"The General Hospital has a huge furnace where they burn up their old surgical body parts, old kidneys, amputated arms and feet, dead babies, whatever. So we just send the carcasses over there to the Gen."

"Do you have to burn them?"

"Well, it would be somewhat unseemly to have ten or twenty dustbins full of dead boons out on the curb. People might complain."

"Would it be possible to get some hands and feet for me?"

"What the fuck do you want with that? And how many?"

"They're good, *muthi*. You tie them to a pole and set them up next to your beehives. Keeps the bad spirits away."

"All right, I'll ask our chaps. How many do you want?"

"As many as you can fit in your truck."

"Ok, then they will have to freeze them and when the fridge is full I'll bring them over."

"Thanks a stack."

It must be remembered that in those days the Professor was not yet a "professor," but a perennial student. His professor then was a snobbish Free State Israeli who affected a knowledge of French and never got blood on himself. One day, garbed in a three-piece pinstripe suit, he ventured into the Professor's laboratory, who knows why, and inexplicably opened the fridge, which by then had a good forty hands and feet piled on top of each other. He closed the fridge and asked the young experimenters, "Need I even ask who set this lot up? Are we selling parts here?" Silence prevailed for a moment. He singled out the Professor. "Young man, do you realize how many laws are being broken?"

"Not really. Many?"

"You'll be disenrolled by this time tomorrow."

So ended the Professor's academically sanctioned career forever. From that point on, he went his own way, though his preoccupation with simian variant research gave him direction. To do it all properly he would need seed money. That's where his old friend, Fiemies Moofat, came in.

In the young Professor's neighborhood there had been a grand home that came to be called Moofat's Castle, modeled on the Kronborg Castle at Elsinore in Denmark, where Hamlet's ghost is said to walk the parapets. The Professor lived with his family across Valley Road in a house that was to be the Castle's servants' home. It had fourteen foot ceilings on the first and second floor, a grand staircase, twelve-foot oak pocket doors and more. There were several tunnels under the house that were blocked off but were rumored to lead to the Castle.

The family that built the Castle and lived in it only thirty years, sold it to the Moofats in a vandalized and run-down condition. Prior to the scheduled renovations and before the family moved in, the Professor entered the Castle and found the place infested with do-nothings and vandals busy smashing the contents. There was a grand piano thrown down one of the staircases and Delft tile work torn off the walls and crushed underfoot. Pulled down from the ceiling were chandeliers made of Civil War rifles. On the floor, broken to pieces, there was a blunderbuss of the Revolutionary

War carved with the soldier's name and date.

Moofat, a wealthy importer, his wife, Sorrell, and their two children moved in shortly after renovations were complete. Their son, Fiemes, born without bones in his legs, lived since childhood in a small cottage at the edge of the woodlot, built to look like a smaller version of the Castle, about a hundred yards from its rear entrance. Family servants brought him meals and took care of his toileting, medical, personal and other needs. He had a little wheeled contraption his father had designed that allowed him to get around well enough. It was a bit like a wicker chair that moved, battery powered, with a canvas roof to keep the rain off. He looked silly in the thing, the Professor thought, with his boneless legs dangling down in front like a pair of stockings.

In summer, when he and Fiemies were home from St. Cuthbert's Academy and had plenty of free time, the Professor read to his handicapped friend for hours every day. Fiemies was capable of reading himself, but loved to close his eyes and just listen. There was always something of interest in the Castle's vast library. Sea tales were a particular favorite, as were arcane medical texts like Blumgarten's *Materia Medica*. As soon as the Professor had read the last lines of *Moby Dick's Epilog*, Fiemies would say, "Start over, start over," or, "*Two Years Before the Mast!* That one I love. Even Melville loved it." When dull medical texts were read, Fiemies kept his eyes open and took careful notes.

At summer's end, when schooling at St. Cuthbert's resumed, Jacob and Sorrell decamped for the warm breezes of the Yucatán. Fiemies wouldn't see them until spring. The Moofat daughter, whose name the Professor never learned, was also an invalid, probably a victim of infantile paralysis. The only glimpse he ever had of her was when he was perched on the Castle wall one day eating a tongue sandwich. He happened to be looking at a chimney swift swooping past a third-story window when a maid suddenly threw the curtains open and he saw the girl lying in an iron lung. She must have been about twelve or thirteen. She turned her head toward the sun and struggled for a smile. The poor thing died before she was twenty.

After a year-long exchange of letters and telephone calls, Fiemies and the Professor took passage aboard the *Amber Princess* on a voyage from Calcutta to Phnom Penh. Somewhere in the Bay of Bengal, near the Burmese coast, a small flotilla of boons washed out of the stormy north. Some were taken aboard to be examined. Others were left to ride the waves wherever they took them and seemed quite content to do so.

"They're all females," the Professor told Fiemies. "They float from port to port, looking for males to mate with, but there aren't any. This is where my research will lead, to better boons."

Fiemies set the brake on his old wheeled wicker chair as a wave broke across the deck. "Who could have guessed boons would come along the way they did?"

"I, for one, did not foresee it," the Professor said.

Fiemies packed his pipe, pressing the cherry-scented tobacco down hard with a yellowed thumb. "One can see the wisdom of perhaps using them in certain ways, as long as they're with us, for the good of all," he said.

"I suspect so," said the Professor. "The trade is brisk in the Fertile Crescent already. But I tell you, if we move toward importing them, we've got to be very careful. Cautious traders always look into a boon's mouth, you know, before sealing the deal. If her gums are blue, she's a peaceful sort, maybe lazy, but good humored and safe with the children. She would not make a good yardman or a butler. A blue gum's place is the kitchen. If her gums are red, it's *caveat emptor* all the way. A red gum is just as likely to cut your throat with a corn knife as serve you a slice of pie. Factories employing too many red gums are plagued with trouble all the time."

All this pleased Fiemies, who was always on the lookout for things new and unusual. "This is nevertheless something worth exploring. It sounds like it could be lucrative."

The Professor shook his head. "Right now there is a ban on importing brood, but as their price is about two and half times higher than only a year ago, a healthy trade remains."

At the time, smuggled Burmese boons were posing a threat to the law enforcement agencies in district headquarters. The porous coastline in the Bay of Bengal, shared by both countries, was hardly any hindrance to the smuggling gangs, who were active throughout the year. In recent months, though, in the face of police raids, the smugglers had been slathering their boons with a coating of mud to look as if they had been collected from local fields, making the job of the police more difficult.

In the fall of '88, the Professor was in Kuching, an administrative capital on the Island of Borneo, known as the "Gateway to Borneo." He had been told that good quality breeding boons could be gotten there at a decent price. The locals liked to say that it rained in Kuching every yesterday, today and tomorrow. Not ordinary rain, but of a cast yellow as bile and warm as piss as it struck the skin. If the Professor left his sweaty shoes beside his bed at night, they would be covered in green mold when he got up. He kept a spray bottle of bleach on the bedside table for killing mold wherever he saw it.

Sitting at a table in the Cat's Town Bar, drinking sambuca and plum juice, with the sounds of rattling knives and screaming Muslims outside, the Professor was reminded of his last visit to Katmandu. He had arrived in the middle of a civil disorder and was confined to his hotel for three days. Aside from policemen beating up Maoists and Maoists beating up policemen, the only other real excitement was being awakened every morning by the diabolical cackle that emanated from the loud-hailers of a mosque, then looking out of the window up to the peaks of Everest and Annapurna, and then down to streets where there was a full raging battle between street dogs and crows over possession of the one-meter high bank of Katmandu garbage.

The Professor said to the bartender, "Listen to that. It sounds like a fantasia written by Górecki."

The bartender seemed not to understand. "The Greek? The Spaniard? The painter they called El Greco?"

"No, no. Górecki. The Polish composer they called Henryk Mikolaj Górecki."

"You want a drink, Professor, sir?"

"Yes, what have you got that's strong. Very strong. I have a painful procedure to do. You best not look."

"I give you some arrack. You will like it. Extra strong. We sometimes call it lion's milk."

After a decade of buying *vrot* red wine at outrageous prices in Africa, the Professor was looking for a change. "If you say so, mate."

The milky-looking drink was bitingly alcoholic and smelled of rotted fruit. "Excellent," the Professor said. "Give me the whole bottle…. And, bartender, let me ask you a question. Have you heard of the French philosopher, Jean Paul Sartre?"

The bartender shook his head. "I don't think so, sir."

"It doesn't matter. Sartre said, and I think I'm quoting closely, 'Consciousness is a being, the nature of which is to question its own being, that being implying a being other than itself.' Don't you think this is why a body can stay alive long after consciousness is dead?" The bartender shrugged, then blew his nose into a bar rag. "Nevermind, then," the Professor said, lifting his second arrack, preparing himself for the procedure.

After drinking half the bottle, he probed around his never-healing leg wound with a pair of jewelers' forceps until he felt a sliver of bone. "I got it!" he yelped. The bartender, thinking the Professor was having a heart attack, rushed to him. "There it is," the Professor said. The bone fragment was about two centimeters long. "A first class relic. I must be careful, though. Don't want to flood the market. Also I do not want to compete with St. Theresa of Avila who is spread, piecemeal, all over fucking Europe." His cackling laughter vibrated the bottle of arrack so much, it scuttled an inch or more over the damp tabletop.

"I have never seen a thing like that," the bartender said, grimacing at the site of the Professor's seeping wound. The odor of it sickened him and already it was attracting flies. He felt light headed.

"Bit of a mishap at university," the Professor said. "Hit by a car. They found my calf on the bumper a day and a half later, full of maggots. The wound's never healed. It's been producing these relics all along. I keep them in little phials in my medicine cabinet. Some day I'll build a proper reliquary."

The bartender shook his head and went to the public telephone.

"Who are you calling?" the Professor asked. "I hope not the Pope." The cackling again moved the bottle.

"A tuk-tuk, sir, for you. It is almost time to close."

"Just a minute. Just a minute. I'd like to ask you something. I'm told good boons are available here, breeders. I'm quite interested in getting one. Do you know of any contacts?"

"I don't think so, sir. It's not legal to import them, or sell them."

The Professor held out a hundred dollar bill. "It's American, my man. One hundred."

The bartender wasted no time jotting an address on a napkin and exchanging it for the Professor's hundred. "Go to this place. It is my uncle. He has one or two to sell."

The Professor staggered some on his way to the tuk-tuk, which carried him to the uncle's address. It was a long ride and he had sobered by the time he arrived. "Stay, please," he told the driver. "I'll be back shortly."

The concrete block building housed a poultry seller. The Professor went in warily. A hairy, paunchy man sliced off the head of a goose with a swift knife pass and let it drop into a basket, then hung the body to bleed.

"Excuse me," the Professor said. "The young man at the bar, he said you might have a boon for sale."

Without responding, the man scalded the goose to loosen its feathers before dropping it into a round rotating steel barrel with many rubber fingers lining the inside. As the drum spun, and the goose whirled around, the force of the rubber fingers jiggled the feathers off.

"Excuse me," the Professor repeated, more insistently this time. "I understand you have boons."

The man pointed to swinging door. "In back. If you want, five-hundred."

"Thank you. I'll have a look."

In a dimly lit corner, a boon sat on a stool weaving a basket. She looked old and undernourished. Her eyes were dull and tired, and she smelled quite bad. The Professor was certain this wasn't the one for him. It looked like her breeding days were well past.

"Sorry to disturb you," the Professor said and returned to the tuk-tuk.

Tiring of the rain in Kuching, and with recent news that Fiemies would back his venture with substantial funds, the Professor cut short his stay and went over to Long Semado in Sarawak to visit Yaya, a retired Iban head man and old friend who had been to school once under Scots missionaries, and was quite well educated, if unevenly and with notable gaps. He was covered in tattoos, face to feet, and the three on his fingers indicated he'd personally taken at least that many heads in his heyday. Despite all that, he would be an invaluable resource in providing brood-stock connections in that part of the world.

To get to Yaya's longhouse, the Professor flew to Lawas, the sin capital of northern Borneo, where he stayed the night in a run-down motel with dozens of flying roaches in the room. In the morning he went to the duty-free store and bought a bottle of arrack smuggled in from the nearest anchorage at Labuan. Then it was five hours in a limber pedal-lorry up mountains of mud, pure, sentimental mud, not one rock, stone or boulder. After that it rained and he waited three days for the road to dry off enough to move again.

Yaya told the Professor that the headmen of the various Iban kompongs, or villages, had been charged with setting the price a prospective husband must pay to the bride's family, the *lobola*, at either three water buffaloes or three croc hides. Meanwhile the Muslim Malays in parliament in Kuala Lumpur were lobbying to take away headmen's rights on the grounds that they were not Muslims, but animists, and that they were usually too soused to perform their duties and were not entitled to civil servant pensions.

"None of this is true," Yaya said. "When I was in the shrinking business, I did quality work. When a head is done right, you recognize the person. The face retains its features. Nowadays all you find on the market are baby heads, not shrunken, not smoked, complete fakes. Now I deal in skulls only."

With head hunting a thing of the past, and with his revered stature as an elder, Yaya had time on his hands and had taken up cockfighting. He had a tough rooster named Greenking. The Professor went along to watch a match. Within the first minute Greenking charged across the pit and, with one swipe of his gaffe, gouged half an eyeball out of his opponent, a slutty little rooster from Spaho. Two minutes later Greenking sliced the Spaho slut's throat, cutting it clean across. To the Professor, the blood rushing out of the slut's headless hole looked just like a recirculating fountain of *vrot* wine. Greenking tried to peck at it but Yaya didn't allow him to ingest inferior blood.

That evening, over glasses of arrack, the Professor asked about boons. He said he wanted one for study purposes.

"I can get you all the brood you want."

"No, I want a mature one."

"Not so easily done," Yaya said. "But I will put out the word."

Intending to travel to Sibu in a few days to look over a piece of property, the Professor had time on his hands and offered to help local Ibans with their harvest. But he quickly twisted his left knee operating a defective hay rake through the rice field just down the road from Yaya's longhouse. He hobbled there in intense pain and couldn't walk for few days. He just lulled and hurt in an old spare cane hammock in Yaya's kitchen. It was as close to traction as one could find in Long Semado. Yaya did his best to nurse him and tried forcing more and more betels into his mouth until his visual field was little more than a moiré nightmare and he was spitting the nuts at Yaya's wife's Amporn hens as they scurried around the kitchen mat. Yaya then infused him with ginkgo, gwattle and kwinto and forced him to drink a concoction of Zhonglu and Chongqing Nanlu. Shortly after these *muthis*, as Yaya had assured him he would, the Professor fell into deep and restful sleep as the evening crickets began their songs.

Arriving at Sibu, a beautiful little port on the Rajang River, the Professor invested a good portion of his savings in a property just outside the city, where he would set up a clinic for the study of simian variants, particularly boons. There was a small wooden house with a sturdy garage that would serve well as a laboratory, and a little pond full of koi. A shed on the other side of the pond where pigs had been kept by previous owners would be perfect for keeping the boon he would have as soon as one became available to Yaya.

Once he had settled into the house, the Professor established a routine. He awakened each day at 4:30, drank boiled Sumatran coffee, smoked two or three Players cigarettes, then took three pills for hypertension, one for emotional balance and one for dengue fever, which did not work. All of these pills were supposed to reduce or kill his libido but they hadn't.

Then it was time to strike the bellows pose for awhile, according to the method of Yogi Vithaldas. The pose is called the bellows because the breath moves in and out vigorously with a sound like a blacksmith's bellows. The Professor first assumed the lotus pose, then let his left hand fall easily into his lap. For the rest of the pose he followed the Yogi's instructions: he inhaled through one nostril while holding the other one closed with the fingers of the right hand, its thumb extended. The first and second fingers were bent into the palm while the third and fourth were kept straight.

When the nasal cleansing was finished, the Professor moved on to Dhoti Kriya. First, having earlier drawn a glass of water from the kitchen, he placed in it a long piece of gauze, then resumed the lotus position. Vithaldas taught that stomach cleansing was one of the six processes of purifying the body. To achieve the cleansing, the Professor had to swallow the long piece of wet gauze, in increments, its entire length. When the gauze reached the stomach, he would begin to rotate the muscles surrounding the rectum, which gives a cleansing massage to the stomach and removes accumulated mucous.

Afterward, in a calmer state, and with a fly swatter close at hand, the Professor would sit outside in the sun, where he could better see, and check the relic factory in his leg for bone fragments.

One morning, in the middle of his bellows pose, the postal van arrived with a note from Yaya saying he'd found a suitable boon. It would come by railcar the following day.

Full of anticipation, the Professor was at the station an hour early. He smoked a Player's and paced the cobbled platform, stopping often to glance at his watch, then look up and down the track, hoping for an early arrival.

When it did arrive, porters unloaded a sizeable bamboo box, placed it on a dolly and hefted it into the bed of the Professor's truck. Through the box's narrow slats, one could see the boon's bright eyes peering out. The porters were uneasy. One of them asked the Professor, "What is that inside?"

"My boon," the Professor said. "All the way from Borneo."

Once uncrated and settled into her quarters, the boon slept

more than two days. The Professor sat beside her on a nail keg at intervals, taking her temperature, probing her vaginal aperture with a tongue depressor, measuring her arm spread, snipping samples of her hair and other procedures, then writing down his observations.

In a few weeks, the boon was wide awake and full of energy. She took a fancy to eating the algae from the pond behind the laboratory building and watching the koi swim about. After some deliberation, and a good deal of time spent in her company, the Professor decided to name her Ruthie.

During the rainy season, from November to February, rheumatoid arthritis inflamed the Professor's lumbar region, forcing him to spend more time than usual compiling his field notes and random observations:

§ An incipient, but not visible beak, quite avian, yellow-orange in color, lying among labial folds between and below the nares. On a few occasions, when enraged, she has everted the beak to inflict bites on my hands.

§ I often find her wandering in the oak grove, dragging her fingers along the ground, sweeping up acorns like rug dirt and eating them.

§ Complains effusively when her radio fails to work under water.

§ Has eaten all the snails on the clinic grounds.

§ On Sunday morning she shrieks in unison with the little pagoda bell down the way.

§ Can be can be quite good company when she's taken a glass or two of arrack.

§ Gave me a canto she'd written on the back of an envelope:

    Oh great scrofulous sow
    Anjing busok
    Decaying pig
    Putrefatto maiale
    Bleed jy nog?

    Will you feed the moofish well
    And drive the hero home?

    Joyous gerrids ringing
    Burmese bells, slushing
    In the stink gat.

    Oh where has Oswald gone
    Leaving bones hither and yon?
    The hero's buffalo amiss
    Seeking sclerogibbid giblets
    Swathed in gelastocorid gravy.

    The egrets have flown,
    Home to the hero's grave.
    Wings filled with splinters
    Of flume.

    Gerald the traveler,
    Across leper's yellow pages,
    Gunked to the hilt.

    Unbridled misery of
    Sparrow quarrels
    Winging over the hero's grave.

§ I read in the Proceedings that a boon in Sampit, after repeated copulations with local volunteers, farrowed months later, resulting in the first known male offspring. For a few months, he appeared healthy and vigorous, but succumbed to plague before the year was out.

§ My own problems becoming severe. Amongst the more worrying is clutch-slip, a bizarre neural disorder with associated atrophy of the anterior left thigh muscles. In practice it means that when I drive my little Datsun *bakkie* backwards up a slope, as to exit my drive, the interplay of petrol foot and clutch foot goes *vrot* and I cannot maintain the clutch at the right level to keep the engine going and everything kills and I start again.

§ She completed a difficult canto today. She always reads them to me until I'm satisfied. The more I like them, the more she clicks her beak:

Pange linqua gloriosa,
Rancid paté d'adipocère
Of Teresa de Cepeda y
Ahumada.

Incorrupt vagina weevils'
Snouts clogged with thrush
Playing the waatlemoen series
For the hero.

Cloud-hunting in Brinchang
Yielding the fruits of Fujimori
Riding his llama.

In order to keep Ruthie in good health, the Professor established a biosecurity program that would prevent the introduction of diseases into the premises where she was kept. No source of infectious agents would be allowed entry. In cases where it was necessary to bring other simian variants to the lab, they had to be from an established disease-free source, and would be quarantined for observation before gaining entry. Potential carriers of infectious material such as people, trucks, poultry crates and equipment would be denied entry unless appropriate disinfection measures were taken. The Professor planned to change clothing and boots and use disinfectant foot baths upon entering the premises or buildings. He would seek to minimize environmental stresses which could cause Ruthie to become susceptible to infections by making sure to provide her proper housing, management, ventilation and nutrition.

A reported outbreak of Boon Plague in Kuching was worrisome. It was an acute, contagious, highly fatal disease caused by a herpes virus. Affected boons showed sluggishness, incoordination, shaking of the head, twisted neck, matted hair and greenish-yellow, bloody diarrhea. Dead ones, commonly found on their backs, paddling their legs, often had blood-stained hair around the vaginal aperture and blood dripping from their nostrils. Eruptive lesions of the mucous lining of the esophagus and intestine were also noted. Sometimes, necrotic plaques appeared in the mouth. The liver was enlarged, copper colored and easily crumbled.

Another danger facing the Professor's boon were toxins, particularly aflatoxin, a mold that grew on cereal grains and oilseeds in wet harvest conditions. Even small amounts produced mortality. And boons with access to stagnant ponds where decaying organic matter like animal carcasses was found, could consume Clostridium botulinum. Botulism caused a progressive flaccid paralysis of the neck called limberneck. Two days later, she would be comatose or dead. Other likely sources of toxins included the deadly ricin in castor beans, the erucic acid in rapeseed meal and rat poisons that contained Warfarin, an anticoagulant. Were Ruthie to consume just a cupful, she could bleed to death the next time she stepped on a nail or swallowed a razor blade.

And more, the Professor's latest post contained various scholarly journals and a fascinating and illustrated account of yaws cases among boons. What a frightful disease, he thought. They first develop frambesioma or 'mother' yaws on the buttocks and legs acquire a thin yellow crust. In time we see feet crippled with sores, producing a remarkable crab-walk. And in the fullness of time a gangosa may obliterate the lower part of the head, making a humanoid funnel lubricated by nasal discharge and into which peanuts could be pushed.

The Professor went to see Fiemies in Jinghong, home of the Water Splashing Festival. Moofat had written to say he wanted to talk over some business ideas. Their initial meeting was held in a rice-papered room of the Burmese Bell factory.

Moofat wheeled himself to the table, followed by Fiona, his personal assistant. "Professor, it is nice to see a friend. I have been here so many years avoiding the desert sands. Thank god for Jinghong during this desert of democracy."

"How goes your health, Fiemies?"

"Never too well, my friend, but look at this." His assistant, Fiona, lifted Moofat's terrycloth skirt. "I've got a nice hydrocoele in my scrotal bag. Turn off the lights and show him, Fiona."

While Fiemies held the bag up in the dark, Fiona shined a flashlight on the hydrocele, which lit up like a light bulb. "It's my latest party trick," he said.

"You wear it like the distinguished flying cross," the Professor said, and recommended a series of homeopathic medicines which Fiemies declined on the grounds that "no hydrocoele, no fun for anyone."

They got down to business after a few tumblers of arrack. Fiemies said, "Let's put boons aside for the moment. I think the two of us will do well in the faux-relic trade. My approach is quite dramatic. Using the latest molecular techniques, my people have procured an adequate specimen from Frances Cabrini's tomb and have extracted very good runs of DNA from it. Cabrini was in the class of 1917 so there has not been a total rot."

The Professor remarked, "No one has yet published a thorough inventory of Teresa de Cepeda y Ahumada. And, also, it is not known whether she was 5- or 6-fingered, so there is room for speculation and parlay in future. They say the coffin lid was smashed, and the smell of dampness and mildew was pungent. Her clothes had fallen to pieces and the body was covered with soil that had sifted into the coffin, yet she was as fresh and whole as at the hour of her death. After she was washed and dressed in clean clothes, a sweet fragrance spread through the house. After three years, without embalming, Teresa remained in an incorrupt state. She seemed to be napping."

"I'm pleased this topic has arisen," Moofat said. "The morning's post brought a 1658 first edition of Browne's *Hydrotaphia*."

The Professor said, "I'm quite familiar with that classic work. He points out that while we expect to have worms in graves, they aren't easy to find there. He did some digging in churchyards and never found a worm more than a foot deep. Teeth, bones and hair give the most lasting defiance to corruption, he discovered. And that in a body ten years buried he saw a fat concretion, where saltpeter and the lixivious liquor of the body had coagulated into the consistency of the hardest castile soap."

"Indeed," Moofat said. "And he pointed out that after a battle with the Persians, the Roman corpses decayed in few days, while the Persian bodies remained dry and uncorrupted. Bodies in the same ground do not uniformly dissolve, nor bones equally moulder. The body of the Marquess of Dorset seemed sound and handsomely cereclothed, when they dug him up after seventy eight years and found him as fresh as an edelweiss."

"If we're going ahead with this, we simply must step up and secure a reliable supply of bones," the Professor said.

"Make a note of that, Fiona," Moofat said. "Bones, bones and more bones."

"Perhaps I know of a mother lode," the Professor said. "I took a quick trip to Phnom Penh and then to Choeung Ek where I had tea with Khmer Rouge notables. I toured a commemorative stupa filled with skulls of Pol Pot's victims. And of course there was a box for tourist contributions in cash. Pol's work was making a fortune from the tourist trade. In the killing fields the executed were buried in mass graves. Apparently, bullet killing is rather expensive when you need to kill so many, one of the notables told me, so Pol Pot's men killed them using hammers, axe handles, spades or sharpened bamboo sticks."

Fiona used a long-handled tweezers to pick little flakes of dead skin from Moofat's muskrat waistcoat. He said, "Inasmuch as any Latin Scholar can fake the documentary requirements necessary for the relic trade, you must realize that with those notables on our team, you and I could simply enjoy Jinghong's many pleasures without all of the pus and guts."

"Yes, the Professor said, "Pol Pot's collection is vast and there are so many bones that the relic business parallels that of diamonds, which only retain value through controlled release on the market."

"And how is Ruthie, that variant of yours?"

"She's taken up smoking my cigarettes. It annoys me to no end. And she writes very good cantos."

Moofat said, "It doesn't surprise me. They're getting quite sophisticated. My Burmese friends tell me they've got some talented new generations showing plenty of chops on the vibraphones."

"And I read in the Proceedings that the Germans have engineered a very large strain, good for heavy lifting. One got loose and has been observed in Wurzburg eating algae from the pond in front of the Biozentrum."

Fiona said, "Professor, perhaps the meeting should adjourn. Fiemies looks very tired."

As the Professor stood up to go, Moofat yawned. "Professor, before you leave and before I forget, the next time you're in Brinchang, pay a call on the Bishop. I hear he has some proprietary information he wants to share."

"I will certainly do that, Fiemies."

"He's a huge player in the trade."

On returning to Sibu, the Professor reached his laboratory well past dusk. He went in and slumped into his chair, exhausted from his travels. There was in the post the new edition of the Bristol Stool Scale, a medical aid designed to classify boon feces into seven groups for diagnostic purposes. The form depended on the time it spent in the colon, and could indicate certain medical conditions from constipation to cholera. There were seven types: hard lumps, like nuts, difficult to pass; sausage-shaped with nibs; like a bloodwurst with surface cracks; like a snake, smooth and soft; pasty blobs with clear cut edges, passes easily; fluffy pieces with ragged edges, mushy; and no solid pieces, entirely liquid.

After a few days of rest, the Professor sat at his old typewriter and pecked out a few notes and two of Ruthie's cantos:

§ The investigation of the digestive organs of different boon types, in which I have been engaged for many years, has led me imperceptibly into an enquiry respecting how they use the lower portion of the intestines, which are arranged so that what passes through must remain quite a long while, perhaps months, before movement is seen. This leads one to believe that the algae undergo change as they linger in Ruthie's colon, and further nourishment is being extracted.

§ I see in the Proceedings that a necrotizing infection (fascitis) that involves the soft tissues of the genitalia has occurred in a small number of otherwise healthy males who have copulated with boons, though a clear cause/effect relationship has not been established.

§ Disturbing news. Must watch for the following:

*Fever and lethargy, which may be present for 2-7 days.

*Intense genital pain and tenderness that is usually associated with edema of the overlying skin.

*Increasing genital pain and tenderness with progressive erythema of the overlying skin.

*Dusky appearance of the overlying skin; subcutaneous crepitation.

*Obvious gangrene of a portion of the genitalia; purulent drainage.

§ The peculiar smell of boon feces, which borders so closely on that of putrefaction reminds me of adipocere, which consists primarily of fatty acids produced by postmortem chemical changes to body fat.

§ Two of Ruthie's newest cantos:

Sante Augusto Pinochet
Ora pro nobis
Sante Francisco Franco
Ora pro nobis.

Rogate my yo-yo
And the broken chicken
Eating jumping beans.

The hero walking his lobster
Bowed ceremoniously to
The boon.

Emerita talpoides flew
Deeply into the sand
Holding the litanies safe.

Sancta Gerda Munsinger,
Ora pro nobis,
Sancta Sui hu Zuan
Ora pro nobis.

§ Although I always try to be kind to her, still I harbor some resentment toward Ruthie who, in a spectacular error of judgment, gave my fine sliver of St. Ansanus to a stray dog. I remember the time when, before they were sainted, Ansanus and Maxima were scourged, which took out the latter. It required oil-boiling for the former. When Ansanus was submerged in bubbling oil, crackling and popping sounds were heard as moisture from his thorax reacted with the oil.

§ When Ruthie got her leakage all over my settee last spring, I decided to research the matter of naturally absorbent materials. I asked Yaya to breed luffas, three species: Luffa acutangula (ridge luffa), L. aegyptica (mummy luffa) and L. operculata (sponge luffa). Once growing, he worked out their nutritional needs and after harvesting, he retted them in clean rain water until the odour was gone. Then he sun-dried, graded and tested them. Ruthie is an ideal test subject for this because she is known to emit oozing, seeping, and dripping substances from the mouth, rectum and vaginal aperture, all foul smelling. Yaya came to Sibu and fitted her out with a luffa for each condition. And, as an extra precaution, I fitted her to a series of catamenial sacks. First, I thoroughly sponged her with tincture of green soap, applied cracked ice and sprinkled her with ergot, then sacked her well in full incandescence. This cat sack has a double-acting spring intended to girdle the waist and prevent epileptic relapses.

§ I was taking a shortcut through a field on my way to the night market in Sibu for a tub of butter, when I discovered a human penis in the dirt. I searched the area for the rest of the body, or other remains, but none were found. After I removed and preserved some larvae from the penis, the organ was sent to a forensic science laboratory for examination. Entomologists who examined the larvae thought the circumcised member may have been there as long as four days before being found. I did not know whether the victim had been alive or dead when the organ was severed. Hospitals and funeral homes knew nothing of the case.

When he was in Jinghong to meet with Moofat again, the Professor walked along Glotus Street to the money-changer's stalls next to the lorry park for hay farmers. After changing his money he strayed into the Do Drop Inn for a glass or two of arrack. Moofat was there, having his second round of angostura and gin. His meerschaum, clutched between his teeth, was yellowed from the local tobacco they call twak. Fiona sat next to him and held up his lifeless legs. Moofat was scratching himself through his woolens, eyes closed, off in his own world.

The Professor joined them. "Well, Fiemies, I thought I'd find you here. How do you do?"

"I have been in this jungle so many years I'm turning green. I always feel ... bufonious."

"Quite right, Fiemies. It's the arsenic in the drinking water."

"I tell you Professor, I sent a letter to the Frog, who croaked for your sins. He is the wheel, of which we all are cogs. The world is His swamp, and we are His frogs."

"Perhaps so, Fiemies. I am not sure."

"But, if you think about it, Pharaoh called for Moses and Aaron, and said, 'Intreat the Lord, that he may take the frogs away from me, and from my people; and I will let the people go;' but, in Pharaoh's estimation, the croaking frogs, which came up from the banks, were mean sorts of adversaries."

"I take the view that stone cows are not gods, and don't hear prayers. As far as prayers go, who answers the ones not offered to the stone cows?"

"Enough prattle, Professor. As to some business, I've taken your advice and gotten myself a boon. But she's given me nothing but grief. A local farmer impounded her and is demanding a release fee. Apparently she had gone riparian and was seen suffocating fish eggs and killing young mudfish in a hatchery. I suppose it's my responsibility. I think 500 will cover it. I'll send Fiona to sort it all out."

Moofat asked Fiona for a scratch, which she supplied, then fluffed his tulle. He smiled, and in the effort, pissed himself.

"Indeed," the Professor said, "they are the devil to keep in captivity."

"We must find a use for them," Moofat said. "A profitable use."

"It wouldn't be their bones, Fiemies. As soon as they hit the air, they crumble into dust…. Which reminds me, I must tell you, the Pol Pot bone deal is kaput. They have quite a moneymaker in those bones."

Moofat yawned. "We'll find another source."

"Mr. Moofat is growing weary," Fiona said.

The Professor stood to leave. "Good night, then, Fiemies."

"Good night, Professor. Will you join me for lunch tomorrow? In the morning shipment to the kitchens we will be getting a crate of fresh cuttlefish all the way from Finland."

"Splendid. I think that they will be well served with pomegranate gravy."

The Professor tipped the brim of his snap-down cap as Fiona wheeled Moofat to a waiting tuk-tuk.

Last dry season, the Professor traveled across the Gulf of Siam to Bangkok. He'd read in the Proceedings that a gang of renegade boons were suspected in a wave of penis severings. He taxied in a long-tail boat up the Chao Praya river to spend time with Egg Surasak, the foremost penis-restorative plastic surgeon in Thailand. As he waited for the famed surgeon in the Café Lyon, the Professor sipped tea and read an article in the Bangkok Post about the severings.

When Surasak popped into the Cafe, he said, "Good morning Professor," in his gentle Asian way.

The Professor replied: "Egg on you, Egg. What will you have?"

"Oh, it's a warm day, something light. Maybe pad siew and a bubble tea."

The Professor could sense disappointment in Egg. His social life was somewhat limited because those in his pink-gin drinking circles tired of his endless prattle about pearly penile papules, his favourite topic, Fordyce spots, phimosis and pudendal nerve entrapment, not to mention Peyronie's disease. They delighted him as horse races delighted sheiks. He could not get enough.

"For awhile we were sewing up a lot of cases," Egg said. "My colleague, Professor Muangsombot, says that he and I did thirty-three re-attachments only last month, and oodles more were reported around the country. It had become something of a fad. Boons were showing marvelous ingenuity in trying to prevent the offending body part from being reattached. They boiled them, flushed them down the toilet, buried them and even tied them to balloons and let them float away." Egg's advice to the male population: "If you have a boon, there is the chance it will run amuck and cut you, so always carry a Thermos to put the severed organ in and keep my name and number on hand."

"As you know, Doctor Surasak, from our correspondence, I am keen to observe one of your re-attachments. I do have a boon and even though she's a blue gum, it's always a concern."

"Come along," Surasak said, "I'm doing one this morning. Normally, three or four. There's been a lull of late. Either the boons are becoming more tolerant, or the men are fucking one another to save a bit of money."

The Professor and Dr. Surasak went along to the clinic. Mr. Numthwaite, Surasak's first patient, was tapped in the usual way with a shunt in the gaping wound. The severed penis lay in a tray of salted ice. Surasak trickled a stiff quantity of claret and Bristol water into the puncture, but on withdrawing the perforator, instead of lymph, nothing but a thick, ropy gelatinous fluid issued out. Two gallons of it were immediately drawn off and half this amount of claret and Bristol water injected instead. "This," Surasak told his assistants, "you'll do tomorrow and continue daily until the whole contents should be discharged, although I'm afraid that a total discharge could lead to syncope. In any event, Numthwaite will go cockless for the rest of his life."

Then there was the matter of the autopsy of Mr. Hasiloglu, whose boon had snipped off his penis with a pair of pinking shears and fed it to guinea hens in the neighbor's yard. In a guilt-fueled attempt to repair the damage, the boon first applied twenty leeches to his perineum, then rubbed cold lotions around the stump, along with a prescription of a tartar emetic, calomel and colocynth. So much blood was lost just after the initial severing and for the next few days as his boon tried to nurse him, he died.

Still, when Surasak made his incision, Hasiloglu's innards suggested the boon may have done him a favor and spared him an agonizing death. There was suppuration of a sizable cyst of the liver communicating with the femoral hernia, gangrene of the gallbladder; extravasation of bile and peritonitis.

"Quite clear this chap would have passed on quite soon anyway," Surasak said. Taking the Professor aside, he whispered, "I knew Hasiloglu. He had been sniffing his boon's thing and beating his meat like it owed him money," then offered an apology. "So sorry there were no re-attachments to see today, but come with me to the postmortem forum."

The forum went on for hours, lulling the Professor into a half-sleep as Surasak reported on five cases of amputation of the penis for epithelioma, a sloughing of penis from strangulation by pressure, two cases of violent inflammation caused by constrictions with steel rings and one case of horn on the glans penis supported by a persistent priapism caused by extravasation of blood into the corpora cavernosa.

F rom the Professor's notes:

§ Two more cantos:

Sugifunctis in extremis,
Hero relics in mechanical amour
Burrow-cramped in chrysidid juice

No two-tiered tomb to
Crush him down and
Break his other arm.

The buffalo tends his
Grave in southern style
Near the great wall.

§ Hearing Ruthie cry out from her pen, I went to
her and gave her a strong anodyne. She was terribly
swollen in the abdomen and probably pregnant. Three
weeks later I again went to her and she had a pricking
pain in her navel with swelling and redness, which
grew into a fulsome boil a few days later. Then I
applied an emollient cataplasm and returned next
morning. On removing the dressings a fetid matter
ensued. I dilated the small sinus with scissors and a
tiny scapula jumped out. Then I extended the orifice
to extract the rest of the fetus. First an arm, a few
ribs, vertebrae, then I proceeded to remove the greater
part of the fetus except the cranium. It was female as
always. When I tugged on it, it broke into shards, one
of which pierced her intestines, letting feces issue
through the navel for a few days. I dressed the wound
with spirituous fomentations and cataplasms. I gave
her injections of fack and warm water and a few
days later I was rewarded when a tibia and fibula
issued from the vaginal aperture. Ruthie has perfectly
recovered and since grown fat.

§ It is reported in the Proceedings that a male was
born of a boon and raised in Iceland. Named Angel,
he has lived to maturity in five years and has a
remarkable career exhibiting himself in medical fora
and symposia for a fee. His home base is St Thomas'
and he is well known in Royal Society circles. Angel's point
of interest is that he is three-legged and completely
without pigmentation. Even short stays in the sun
are prohibited. His third leg is an evagination of

the sacrum, but insensate. The knee is fused, yet he can still flap it under his left thigh and strap it there like a flamingo during sleep. He had another secret as well: two functional hemipenises accompanied by three scrota. His service style must have been a pleasure for his mate because he could begin with one hemipenis, ejaculate and switch to the other one. In one remarkable story about the boon boy, his keepers came home after a long visit to Sampit, having crossed the whole of the Kalimantan on foot, and there in the hen house, the boy was copulating with two hens at the same time. He was covered in blood and feathers, but smiling gaily.

Shortly after the Professor's return from Ulusaktuk, in Alaska, where he had gone to take a census of Arctic boons living among the Eskimos, he went to Yaya's longhouse at Long Semado for a cockfight. Yaya's wife prepared banana worms for lunch and they discussed the Professor's recent visit to the Yukon.

"It's not immediately clear to me how the same species of boon that we find in Borneo can also thrive in that Arctic icebox. And I'm quite struck by how well they've integrated themselves into Eskimo society," the Professor said.

He had brought along a carousel projector and screen to show the photographs he had taken. When the first one was shown, Yaya jumped up in an excited state. "Professor, what is all of the white stuff where the ground should be?"

"Snow, Yaya."

"What is snow?"

The Professor thought for a moment, aware that the last snowfall in Long Semado was 18,730 years before Yaya was born. "Well, Yaya, it is water that is what we call 'frozen,' and is a collection of wonderful configurations that sometimes is very hot, at other times remarkably cold."

"I see, but where are their rice paddies?"

"Yaya, they do not grow rice that near the pole."

"Life without rice is not possible. That is why the Eskimos are a dying breed."

In April, the Professor repaired to Sampit, the site of a recent massacre. Yaya had urged him to look into the availability of bones there. His small plane landed near the site of the massacre, the result of a territorial dispute between two tribal groups. Houses were burned, hundreds were herded into a schoolyard and killed, children included. Heads were lopped off and youths were seen parading around with them as trophies.

The smell of rotting corpses as the Professor disembarked was of the most horrible description. The air was so rich in nitrogen and carbon dioxide rising from the dead, and so lacking in oxygen, suffocation was always a possibility if one didn't hurry away from the airport. A party of gravediggers was very nearly lost, the Professor was told. The last man had been dragged out on his back through two feet of black fetid deposit in a state of insensibility. Rats were everywhere. The Professor recoiled. The stench had affected his gag reflex, and he ran to catch the tram.

After a night's fitful sleep at the Hua Kuok hotel, he went downstairs to meet Yaya for breakfast. "Welcome to Sampit," Professor. "Excuse all the pong in the air. So many bodies all around."

As they ate Tung Poh Yoke, a pig's foot dish with galangal and pork rib soup, one of Yaya's new boons put in an appearance. She was saurian in many ways, like a Permian lizard, the Professor observed. Her extensible dewlaps was covered in spawled crenulations and she had a third breast, centred on her sternum six or seven inches below the other two.

Yaya shouted, "She's a three-hooter from the boreal wealds!"

She was a remarkable figure, only four and a half feet high, hunchbacked, with projecting chest, small legs and arms, large round head, showing only beneath the enormous white hat. Her face was covered with a semicircle of white beard falling low on her breasts.

"She looks quite like a troll," the Professor said. "With a smidgen of leprechaun, too."

"Yes, we call her Brownie. Brownie, meet the Professor."

"I'm very pleased to meet you, Brownie."

"She slept with one of my sons," Yaya said. "And after she had perpetrated this sin her face began to swell. She was terrified and thought she had caught leprosy. She told me she would never sleep with a man again, but in order to keep her oath, she began to abuse little girls." He spit yet another mouthful of betel blood onto the hotel carpet and gave his Brownie a kick in the shins. "Get along now. Go down to the market and get your fill of snails. We have business to do." The boon clicked her beak and bowed effusively while backing out of the restaurant.

"That's quite a nice one," the Professor said. "Almost gracious."

"I mate with her almost every day. It makes the wife furious. Would she be angry if I mated with a dog or a rat? It doesn't follow reason."

"Little does, little does. In my case, Ruthie is resistant, but we get it done sometimes, when I pump her up with arrack."

"Brownie likes plum brandy. I keep a few bottles in the longhouse."

The Professor said, "All very interesting, but we have bones to talk about. There seems to be clear potential here for a bumper crop."

"True. First, though, I have a problem at home. Ever since we gave up head shrinking, we have had this problem of people stacking up corpses in their longhouses just at the door, with the head bent to the east in memoriam. They go *vrot* after a while. And that spoils the rice. Then they get soggy and you can't use a corpse-lifter because pieces fall off. In the old days we saved the heads and ate the rest. No *vrot*. Nice dry heads up on the shelf."

"Perhaps the laws will change."

"Perhaps boons will grow teeth some day, too."

"All that aside, Yaya, what do you think of that big pile of bones out there? Skulls for the scientific supply market, the rest for the relic trade. I smell a small fortune in all that stink. We could make an offer."

"We'll want them to stay in the sun awhile, let the bugs and beetles go to work."

"And fencing. We must keep the dogs out."

"Of course. I wonder who owns those bones?"

"Moofat will know."

"Let's schedule a meeting as soon as possible.

In Kuching to meet with Moofat three weeks later, the Professor and Yaya took a tuk-tuk from Kuching Central out along the river but there was a terrible pong in the air. Yaya said, "I remember once being trapped in a crowded train where I could not move because of the mass of people and their bags. The foul smell was on the attack and I can only hold my breath for about two minutes. I visualized myself trapped in a bubble of putrid and foul green air, wafting through the firmament."

The Professor said, "The closeness of people and the extra warmth more quickly volatilized the chemicals, which created the smell, ensuring that the pong was quickly and generously distributed."

The Professor and Yaya went to Moofat's rooms that afternoon and found him in a standing position, his upper body strapped to a tall wooden fixture that looked like a hat rack. He was stationed before a wood burning stove, making a batch of oil puffs concocted from salt pork fat and puff pastry. "My boon loves these," he said. "She eats them after we couple."

Moofat suggested they break for tea, go to the cemetery to read some epitaphs, then take a lorry to the hotel for an early dinner.

Fiona went along to keep him upright and comfortable on the way. The stop at the cemetery didn't go as planned. There were fresh graves being dug and the gate was locked. Not that it mattered particularly, there was such a fog that day the moldy old inscriptions would have been difficult to see. The party quickly abandoned the cemetery for the hotel.

Yaya asked the head waiter, "What can you recommend today?"

"The grilled kidney is excellent. It leaves a nice taste in the mouth, or the caul cream soup. Or you might enjoy the makchang. In the States they call them chitterlings."

Yaya said he loved intestines and would go for the makchang, depending on how it was prepared, and the kidney, too, very lightly grilled. And a side order of head cheese."

"Yes, sir. Steam-cleaned and lightly-grilled."

Moofat said, "Nicely simmered ears, snout and trotters for me."

"Consider it done," the waiter said, turning his attention to the Professor. "Sir, can we interest you perhaps in a poached rectum, some fried rooster testicles, or even a pendulous pair of boar balls?"

"I think today I'll keep it simple," the Professor said, "the fūqī fèipiàn looks intriguing. What is it?"

"Sliced lung."

"Oh, nice. I'll have that and a vim and vit salad. Some oil puffs on the side."

"And you, Miss?"

Fiona said she had a yen for fish cheek soup, makchang and pizzle salad."

Moofat lit his pipe. "Well, I have had memorable meals here. There was the time that American writer, Norse, visited and told us his extraordinary cure for wounded intestines that had fallen out of a split abdominal cavity."

"I do remember that," Fiona said. "As a last resort, he ran them through a gut-cleaning machine until they glistened with joy and exuberance, then pushed them back in with his hands."

"And survived," Moofat added.

The Professor yawned. "So sorry, not much sleep last night. Troubled dreams. Hard to shake them."

Yaya said, "Every morning's awakening is also a forgetting. How could nature be so wasteful as to let such rare and strange parables go unnoticed and uncollected? If dreams are supposed to be instructive in one's life, why do we so readily forget them?"

"I suspect," Fiemies said, "that dreams are really private communications between the mind and the body. They're not intended for conscious use at all."

When the meal was eaten, pipes lit, and brandy served, it was time for business.

"You've called this meeting, Professor. What do you have?"

"The Sampit massacre. Surely you've heard."

"Four hundred *vrot* bodies," Yaya said.

Fiona stood behind Moofat combing his hair. "It was all over the news. Horrible thing."

"Who owns the bones?" Moofat asked. "We could get tied up in red tape. Everyone left alive there will want a cut. Nevertheless, there is an urgency to this because a fence will have to be built."

"Yes," the Professor said, "we don't want dogs scattering the bones all over creation or dragging off the heads. There were a lot of severings, a lot of loose heads."

"A shame we can't shrink them," Yaya said. "That's where the real money is. Every Hollywood star would want one for the mantelpiece."

Fiemies reached up and stopped Fiona's combing. "Make a note, Fiona. We'll fly to Sampit and have a look around."

A few weeks later, Yaya cabled the Professor. His grandfather had died and he was despondent. Knowing that Yaya worshiped the old man and would be in dim spirits, the Professor took a trip to Lawas and then south into the mountains to Yaya's village. He had forgotten the path, so went along until he saw a trail of betel nut spit. When his blood quickened, he knew he was there. In the air was the faint smell of granfatherliness that he expected. The Professor had not seen Yaya since Hoyuma Cabahug, his grandfather, had died last November. The old man had not been buried because the constellations were not quite right.

When the Professor went into the longhouse, he could see that Yaya had followed custom. Cabahug was snug in his coffin some three months now. They had put his body in it, well-caulked with dammar gum, and placed it in the rafters of the house. However, they had wisely cut a hole in the bottom of the coffin and thereto placed a piece of bamboo, which extended from the rafters, through the house and about 2 meters into the ground. This served to convey all the putrid moisture from the corpse without occasioning any smell. A wonderful arrangement for that time and clime.

After an afternoon nap at the end of the longhouse, the Professor awoke in a sweat. He saw Yaya sitting on the stoop gnawing a small human tibia. "My dear Professor, what you see in my face is the mental victory, the thumping of human defeat that comes from eating human flesh. Friends brought me some from Sampit, well preserved in salt. Very fresh taste. They came across a baby, about a day old, the offspring of a woman just taken away by traders. It was left under an oil palm, gasping feebly in the full glare of the noonday sun. They awaited its death and the meal that was to follow." He flung the bone into the brush.

"Well Yaya, that may be. But, whether you are eating flesh for spiritual reasons and/or to sate your hunger, I can promise you that, even if it came from a stew with carrots and onions, we can still detect the myoglobin in your pots and feces!"

The Professor retrieved his logbook from beneath the palm-frond pillow he was sitting on and filled his pen with betel juice ink. "Tell me, Yaya, when you shrank heads, what did you do with them? What was the process? If the laws ever change, we should be ready."

"The heads were brought to me by tribal men. I would pay for a good one. But most of the skulls had been smashed to obtain the brains and thus rendered useless for re-selling to the underground markets. Some heads were still moist and had the odor of recent cooking. Some were brought in when rag-pickers found a severed one in a garbage dump."

"Did you then shrink them?"

"Sometimes we shrank. Sometimes we were after the skull only."

"Yes, but what do you do with the head meat?"

"Leave it to the head-boning beetles. They come out of the forest in ravenous swarms when they smell a fresh head. They can strip one clean in three or four days. Then we sun-dry them to get rid of the pong, the stink of death. The sun also bleaches them nicely."

"When did you first begin to eat flesh?"

"The first time was in the Sampit prison. I was doing a year for some sort of swindle I was accused of but hadn't done. 'Round up the usual suspects,' you know. Every other day I heard someone looking at a new prisoner and saying, 'Shall we kill him for the evening meal? He is tender and fat, the prison is overcrowded, and we are very hungry.' We cooked someone every few days."

"Tell me, did you cook the heads?"

"I don't do goats and I don't do head meat, thank you." Yaya took an areca nut wrapped in a betel leaf from his scrotal bag pouch and placed it between his lower lip and gum.

"What does human flesh actually taste like?" the Professor asked.

"Well, the taste of people meat varies. It has a nice and distinctive aroma as it cooks. But the taste depends on the life-style of the donor and whether they drank alcohol or preferred sweets or salty things. There is a basis for intrinsic taste, which is amplified by lifestyle. Cooking matters too. There is a huge difference if you cook people meat in an electric kettle or a hot plate. A slow roast is the best. Once my sister axed her husband and then cooked him in a variety of dishes which she fed to her boon."

The Professor closed his logbook. "I suppose that's enough for now. Shall we see to burying your grandfather?"

"Yes, yes, as soon as Brownie has the grave dug."

Early in '92, the Professor went to Jinghong, where he was granted an audience with Dr. de Castro, a leader in the field of boon physiology.

The Professor said, "Good morning to you, Dr. de Castro. It is so nice to see you even though there appears to be some chaos out there on the street."

"It's the Water Splashing Festival. The locals go crazy. Everyone gets soaking wet. What brings you to Jinghong?"

"I'm afraid my boon has a Stack's occlusion. I'm hoping you can confirm my opinion."

"I have just examined a Stack's occlusion in a boon. After nine hours a passage was opened, and she voided black liquid excrement, without any infusions of quicksilver. Her bile became fetid on the second day, fetid and yellow on the third, and on the fourth it had the smell of excrement and was flabby."

"She was full of fomentations and glyfters, too."

"Yes. That's a Stack's all right."

"She suffered for a week and on the eighth day began to break wind, retain the clysters, discharge a little feces, and to sleep, though not quietly; and, on the ninth, discharged a very turbid urine. The only cure that worked was a decoction of madder."

"Be wary, Professor. Before she burst open, one of my recent cases suffered iliac passion caused by a palsy of her large intestines. Her evacuations by stool and urine were by no means deficient but her urine was bloody, and she had one thigh and a leg that was edematous. She suffered a delirium and had profuse sweats."

"I think I'll report these cases to Moofat," the Professor said. "The Burmese strain may prove yet to be a medical liability."

"Yes, Professor. I urge you to stop importing them altogether."

A cable from Fiona, on Moofat's behalf, urged the Professor to travel to Brinchang to take the mountain airs and to meet with the Bishop. Having been there on a few occasions of rest and relaxation, the Professor knew the little tourist haven well. It was filled with colorful Tudor-style buildings and, though there were plenty of shops for all goods and sundry, it was crowded with people, cramped with queuing cars and trucks going up to the Ee Feng Gu bee farm or the Boh tea plantation. In fact, during his visits, the Professor had found Brinchang a decidedly unpleasant place. Now he wondered why Moofat was sending him there. Smoky as it was and choking with exhaust fumes, it was no place to take any airs at all.

He was to meet the bishop at the Palace Orienta for a traditional Chinese Steamboat, where diners choose from an array of raw and marinated ingredients to dip into simmering stock.

The Bishop said, "The Steamboat is a brilliant example of the art of interaction, of sharing and socializing. Here we are, sitting around that big steaming wok, feasting on the freshest, most colorful food in the world."

"Certainly tantalizing," the Professor said.

"And they use only organic meats, because it isn't cooked very much," the bishop added as their server presented dishes including blue eye, snapper, halibut and sea bass, along with radish and pickled mustard greens for the dipping sauces, and salted duck eggs.

"Moofat sent me to see you," the Professor said. "May I ask why?"

"Of course. Come to my house tomorrow. We'll talk privately. By the way, Fiemies tells me you have quite a nice boon there in Sibu."

"Yes, I call her Ruthie. She's an interesting one."

"Do you mate with her?"

"On occasion, yes. I'm hoping to fertilize an egg and hatch a male."

"It's a sin you know. The Church recently ruled it so. I must say, I'd love a bit of that myself. Unfortunately it's now a cause for defrocking."

"Perhaps the Church will wake up someday."

"Not bloody likely, Professor. See you in the morning."

"Good day, Bishop."

The Professor hailed a cab and went to the bishop's house after breakfast the next morning. The bishop was at his bath, in his drawers for modesty's sake, and only wearing his amaranth-red zucchetto. The Professor knocked politely, entered, genuflected and kissed the bishop's ring. "Excellency. What is it you have to say?"

"I can tell you in strict confessional confidence that Holy Mother Church is reconsidering its options and redesigning its business plan."

"You mean you are back to selling indulgences?"

"No, not yet. We are doing a market survey to see if all previous indulgence owners have pegged. We cannot risk any more actions for fraud. We are getting a hell of a lot of competition from all these free-range Pentecostal happy-clappers with their guitar services. I wouldn't be surprised if the banjo appears next. Strutin' Jesus, it's a cakewalk if I ever saw one. The thrust of our new business model is neobaptism."

"And that is …?"

"By decree we'll revoke all first baptisms. Everyone will need to have it done again or face excommunication."

"And presumably, eternal fires as well."

"Oh, yes. I thought Moofat would like to be one of the first to know. Who can predict what a stimulus this might be to the relic trade."

"My thanks, Excellency. I'll get word to Moofat as soon as I return to Jinghong."

When the Professor arrived at the Jinghong airport, Fiona was there to greet him with some news: "Fiemies is hoping to get bones in his legs when a donor becomes available. They're keeping an eye on one of his cousins in Sampit who's ill with some sort of awful crud. When he finally goes, Fiemies will have the surgery. We may see him walk again."

"Let's hope for the best," the Professor said, "but never expect it."

"I should tell you, Professor. Yaya has been here for weeks. Brownie fell out of a tree and cracked her skull on a stump. They're going to give her a nice new metal plate."

"Yaya's boons always get the best treatment. He loves them."

"To a fault," Fiona said. "Come, now. We'll be having supper at the Cai Chun Qing. Their flash-fried dragon shrimp are not to be missed. And the menu is in English."

Fiona showed the Professor to their waiting cab, whose driver displayed a head of quills and feathers. "Be sure to compliment his hair thing," Fiona said. "We'll have a better ride. He's a Dai. One of the minorities. Descendants of the Thai's who lived here once. In fact, Jinghong comes from a Thai word meaning City of the Dawn."

The Professor leaned into the front window. "Very swanky hair you've got, driver, and very creative." He formed a porcupine shape with one hand and quills with the other, then moved the hand through the air like a crawling animal. The driver finally understood and nodded.

Fiona and the Professor settled into the back seat. It was a hot, humid afternoon. A brief shower had fallen a few minutes before. The Jinghong streets that had been blacktopped were steaming. There were piles of garbage like earthworks on both sides, blocking any view of the shops.

"Jinghong has run out of landfill space," Fiona said. "We'll start dumping at sea as soon as Fiemies works out an agreement with the local bosses. Meanwhile, we've got a backlog."

"Nasty pong, too," the Professor said. "There must be bodies in there."

Fiona nodded. "That would be a safe bet. A bad fever has been going around. Dengue maybe. The old are keeling over in pretty good numbers. Some of the bodies are missing organs. Some are in pieces. The surgeons practice on them, apparently, then toss them out. Old people, sick people, condemned criminals."

By the time the taxi arrived at the restaurant, situated in the cleaner, less redolent outskirts of Jinghong, night had fallen. There was a bright gibbous moon rising above the restaurant, which the Professor took to be a good sign.

At the table in a private room, Fiona and the Professor greeted Yaya, who sat next to Brownie and teased her by tapping on her new metal plate with a spoon. Fiemies said, "Welcome to Jinghong once again, Professor. We have things to talk about. Fiona has the agenda. But for now, let's eat."

The table was already set with appetizers and bottles of arrack. The Professor's eye was particularly attracted to the luna moth on toast. Large as a hand, the plump-bodied insect had been opened across a slice of rice cake, slathered with hoisin sauce, and toasted. Yaya enjoyed feeding boiled grubs to Brownie and having a few himself.

Fiona cracked open the shell of a steamed balut and fed the embryo to Fiemies, whose teeth clacked annoyingly when he chewed. "When I get my bones I'm going to take walks," he said. "I'll buy some nice shoes."

As soon as the dragon shrimp and dumplings were eaten and everyone was full of food and arrack, Fiona ordered green tea all around and brought up the first item on the agenda. "The preparation of relics. Should our process be standardized, agreed upon, and set down on paper in some sort of legal fashion?"

The Professor said, "First, I have news from the Bishop. Neobaptism is their latest thing. All old baptisms null and void. Everyone needs to do it again. Perhaps we can swing something along the lines of a little sliver of saint's bone with your baptism, in a nice commemorative package of course."

Moofat shook his head, "Canon law strictly forbids the selling of first-class relics."

"The punishment is light, however," the Professor said. "A Romanian thief who swiped a relic and other religious items from a French church was nabbed in New Jersey and charged with a decidedly mundane crime, filing a false customs report."

Moofat spoke up. "Very good. And if a bribe becomes necessary, the Church is always willing. We'll soon begin releasing our first-class fakes, certified to come from incorrupt saints, those who persistently fail to putrefy. Think of the Blessed Imelda Lambertini, who died in ecstasy during her First Communion in A.D. 1333 at age 11. But there is something fishy here because if you are still loitering in the "blessed bowl" for 700 odd years you cannot be too expert in peeling off that last desperate miracle which gets you through the glass floor. We have a better deal in St. Bernadette Soubirous, who saw Our Lady at Lourdes and who now lies in a glass coffin at her convent in Nevers, France. She is as uncorrupt as they come. There are others: St Catherine Laboure, St Margaret Mary Alacoque, St Agnes of Montepulciano and St Etheldreda come to mind. The last is only a hand, so is only fractionally incorrupt. The rest got lost. But we have a good case in St Withburga and St Isidore, the farmer who married Maria Torribia and just kept ploughing. Then still in the blessed bowl there is a fistfull but I tend to venerate St. Charbel Makhlouf and keep an eye on Eustochia Calafato."

Yaya said, "No one knows why some saints are preserved from corruption while others are not. This is something of a real heavy duty biological conundrum which is a matter apart from the theological/ philosophical problem as to the nature of incorruptibility. Basically we must ask: is incorruptability both necessary and sufficient to constitute proof of holiness?"

"You know what they say," Moofat said. "Where there is dirt there is a system. This is the endlessly nagging concern."

Only a week later Yaya's Brownie passed away of natural causes. When the Professor arrived, Yaya was inconsolable. Out of respect for Yaya and his longhouse companions, the Professor went to the Fifteenth Mile Bazaar to Krokong's coffin factory to get a coffin for Brownie.

Krokong said, "Good morning Professor. I am sorry to see that you are in a business frame of mind. Who died?"

"I am afraid to say that it was Brownie. Died peacefully in her sleep, but prematurely. We expected the Burmese stock to be long livers. We were wrong."

"I knew Brownie well. Would you like to see our range of small coffins or do you have something special in mind?"

"Yes I rather do, Krokong. I remember that you have been hiding a nice teak log for many, many years. I think this occasion calls for a hand-carved teak box, somewhat rounded. And don't skimp, cost is immaterial."

"Professor, consider it done. I shall deliver tomorrow evening if not sooner."

"Thank you, Krokong, you are a very obliging fellow. Just enter a debit on my account."

Before going back to the longhouse, the Professor went to the only telephone in Lawas and arranged for a proper funeral in the Kuching cathedral. The whole longhouse booked the train to Kuching with Brownie on an elevated platform so that she could hear the sea. When everyone had disembarked, enough tuk-tuks were hired to take them all to the cathedral.

Soon Ruthie began releasing specific body parts when these parts were grasped, a form of autotomy. The first time it happened, she was standing on an overturned bucket as the Professor trimmed her nails with a freshly-sharpened paring knife. One of her feet was firmly in his grasp when a fit of laughter threw her off balance and she fell backward. When she did, the foot "snapped" off in the

Professor's hand. It was a ghastly and shocking site at first, yet there was no bleeding and no cry of pain from her. She righted herself and quite calmly replaced the bone in its socket, as if it were a snap-toy, and all was right again. She took a few steps this way, then that, and climbed back onto the bucket.

Only a day or two later, the Professor caught her stealing lard from the laboratory icebox and chased her past the house, around the pond, and finally to the edge of the woodlot, where, when she turned to see where he was, he reached out and took hold of her scruff, which shed its flesh into his hand and she kept on running.

All of this led the Professor to a bit of reading about autotomy in the archives of the Proceedings. In lizards, he discovered, it is the tail that autotomizes, not the digits or limbs. In a few species, portions of skin autotomize, a defense strategy known as "fragile skin." In the terrestrial plethodontid salamanders, tails, digits, and portions of their limbs are sacrificed as a means of escaping predators. Grasp a cricket by the leg and watch it break the limb away with a snap. The sea cucumber will fling its innards at a threatening drum-fish to disorient it, then sidle into hiding and grow new ones.

Like lizards who have evolved tail autotomy as an escape strategy, Ruthie displayed movements of her "bottom" that were intended to attract the Professor's attention away from her more vulnerable top parts. The downy hair there showed sharply contrasting colors and patterns. At the same time the Professor noticed a stereotypic "twitching" back and forth as she positioned herself for a run in the event he attempted to mount her.

But the escape maneuver would be costly, representing a loss of fat and protein, which is needed for regrowth of tissue. During this time, she would remain at higher risk for his predations, as there would be little or nothing else for her to drop. And, her reproductive life would go into hiatus, with gamete production completely halted.

The Professor theorized that autotomy in boons is enabled

by special zones of weakness at regular intervals in the vertebrae below the vaginal aperture. Essentially, she contracts a muscle to fracture the vertebra itself rather than break the "tail" between two vertebrae. Sphincter muscles then contract around the caudal artery to stanch bleeding.

While autotomy was rare in mammals, the Professor knew it occurred in mice, rats and certain other rodents who could slough off the sheath of skin and fur covering their tails. He found this out one day when he was "swing-bonking" a rat against his laboratory wall to kill it. Suddenly, its weight was gone. He heard it thump against the wall and then strike the terrazzo floor. There he stood, with a limp, brown tail-sheath in his hand, watching the rat disappear behind the autoclave.

Consulting the Proceedings in regard to honey bees and autotomy, he found that the stinger tears cleanly away from its body, though the sting shaft keeps moving to embed itself deeper, and the venom sac continues pumping for several minutes. The sting of a queen honey bee has no barbs and does not autotomize, while the genitalia of male drones do autotomize during copulation, and form a "mating plug" which is removed by subsequent drones that mate with the same queen and die in the process. Crabs, brittle stars, lobsters and spiders, can also lose and regenerate appendages. Autotomy also occurs in some kinds of octopus. A specialized reproductive arm, the hectocotylus, detaches from the male during mating and remains within the female's mantle cavity.

More drastic self-preservation strategies were also noted in the Proceedings: A California man amputated his leg below the knee with a chainsaw when it became stuck beneath a tree he'd felled. In Utah, a hiker's forearm was hopelessly crushed beneath a boulder. To get free, he severed it through the elbow with a pocketknife, then broke and tore the two bones apart. An Australian coal miner amputated his own arm with a Stanley knife when he found it trapped beneath his front-end loader when it overturned deep within a coal mine. A New England crab fisherman got his arm caught in the winch during a storm and amputated it at the shoulder with a small axe.

There were even rarer cases where self-amputation had been performed for other purposes. In Florida, a bizarre scam was uncovered involving individuals who cut off their own limbs to collect insurance money. A deranged Jesuit in New Orleans cut his hand off with an electric saw and videotaped the process to, "send a message to the FBI and the media." Evidence suggests the priest was a victim of Body Integrity Identity Disorder, a mental state in which one acts out a compulsion to remove body parts, usually a limb, but sometimes eyes, ears, tongues, even such internal organs as the appendix and the spleen.

Given these facts, the Professor took the precaution to store any and all sharpened objects in his laboratory safe, even kitchen knives from the house. It was one thing for Ruthie to exhibit simple autotomy for the purpose of escaping danger, but quite another if she embarked on a mental trail leading to self-amputation.

Though it was the Professor's fondest hope that Ruthie would be spared any further development along these evolutionary lines and that she would continue in health and safety until the end of her days, it was not to be.

F rom the Professor's Notes:

§ Ubi pus, ibi evacua. Found Ruthie lying in the beak-up posture and saw more than two spoonfuls of stinking pus or corruption, full of liquor puris, run from her mouth after a little coughing. Then, after consulting the Bencao Gangmu, I discovered that her intrauterine body cavity revealed pyometra, an abscessed uterus filled with yellowish-green stinking pus. Her vaginal aperture must have been at some former time very much diseased. The area a finger's length from the anus was contracted to almost a soda-straw size. At the farther end lay a large maggot, near an inch long, with several flies near it. I fear that even with treatment, death may occur.

§ I have begun to milk her to treat her local proliferative fibrogrnaulomatous panniculitis and, to assuage her tormented soul, I swath her in jamlong and feed her qat to quell those mucosal abnormalities. She has suffered extreme lethargy for a week and on the eighth day she began to break wind, then had a clyster, after which she slept, though not soundly. On the ninth day she discharged a turbid urine. There is an opulence of contumaceous whelps amongst the fat depots of the epidural space, which is dotted with spinergy. I did not rejoice in the discovery of degenerative, bulging (as well as thinning) disks and a spinal stenosis.

§ Her cheeks reddened today. I smelled her breath, the best way to diagnose any illness or condition in a boon. It's a bad cold coming, I'd say. Tonight I will add a little red currant jelly to a glass of hot lion's milk before her bedtime, and that should do the job. Maybe I'll also take a pound of gravy beef, cut off all the fat, chop it fine and make her some beef tea. Then I think the best thing to do is to give her a mustard bath. Two tablespoons of mustard per gallon of water. In the basin I'll mash the mustard into a paste, then gradually add it to her bathwater.

§ Found her this morning lying feet up on the kitchen floor, her tail wet with blood. There was hemorrhaging in the anus, heavy and impossible to stanch. I tried mightily with tea towels and hot pads, even my own undershirt, but she was past all hope. She managed a scarcely audible squawk before the last breath came.

After packing Ruthie in ice and having a few oil puffs for breakfast, the Professor went into Sibu and used a public telephone in the market to call Fiemies Moofat.

Fiona answered.

"Ruthie died just now, Fiona. Is Fiemies near the phone? Get him quickly. The connection here is very bad."

"Oh, dear. I'm afraid not. His leg bones arrived from Sampit, the ones he was waiting for. He's under the knife right now."

"Well, wish him the very best luck. And please get word to Yaya that Ruthie is dead. He'll do a dance for her at the very least."

"I will, Professor. I certainly will."

"She was a wonderful subject and companion," the Professor said. "And will be sorely missed."

The Professor had no desire to return home. It had begun to rain and the gloom would depress him. Feeling lethargic, perhaps slightly fevered, he walked along the Rajang Esplanade to the Kingwood Hotel bar, planning to wash away his fever and the shock of Ruthie's passing with arrack. The streets were filled with shoppers. It was the annual Cultural Festival, a celebration of food, music and dance, all quite in contrast to the Professor's funk. And to add annoyance, a spot of blood had appeared on his pants leg. Another relic was emerging.

He sat at the otherwise empty bar and lit a Player's. It was only noon. No drinkers had yet ventured out into the rain. The bartender seemed lost in thought as he sliced lemons with his back to the Professor.

"Hey, there," the Professor said. "What is your name?"

"Sri."

"All right, Sri. Line up a few lion's milks for me, please. There's been a death in the family."

"Sorry to hear that, sir." The bartender poured him three arracks.

"She could be good company," the Professor said, stubbing out his Player's and raising his pants leg.

"Yes, sir."

"Three won't be enough. Leave the bottle."

"Right, sir."

"And you best not look while I do this."

THE EGRETS HAVE FLOWN.
HOME TO THE HERO'S GRAVE.
WINGS FILLED WITH SPLINTERS
OF FLUME.

THE END

GERALD THE TRAVELER
ACROSS LEPER
GUNKED TO
UNBRIDLED
SPARROW
WINGING
OVER THE
HERO'S GRAVE.

ROGATE MY YO-YO
AND THE BROKEN CHICKEN
EATING JUMPING BEANS.

THE HERO WALKING HIS
BOWED CEREMONIOUSLY
THE BOON.

FLIP

REPEAT

A GERDA MUSINGER,
PRO NOBIS.
TA-SUI HU ZUAN

NG THE UTANIES SAFE

THE CAMP

A NOVELLA BY

DAVID OHLE

THE CAMP (& BOONS)
© 2009 David Ohle

ISBN-13: 978-0-9798080-8-1
ISBN-10: 0-9798080-8-1

Art/designs by Derek White.

Published by Calamari Press

www.calamaripress.com

THE CAMP

In 1566 Tycho Brahe, the Danish astronomer, lost his nose in a duel. For the rest of his life he wore a paste-on replacement thought to be made of silver and gold. When his body was exhumed in 1901, however, green marks were found on the skull, suggesting the nose was actually made of copper.

Mimi Chung walked down to the camp's night market to get a few things for a decent supper. Tomorrow would be Jerry's fortieth and she wanted to do something special. The market was open only midnight until dawn and quite crowded at 2 a.m. To make things worse, it was so poorly lit that shoppers bumped into one another

or stepped on each other's feet. Insults were shouted. Scuffles, fights and shoving matches broke out, particularly near the vitamin booth. Campers in that line were often feeling sick and irritable, particularly when the B complex was in short supply, as it had been lately.

There were separate lines for every commodity. In their hurries, the clerks were incompetent with weights and measures and cheated most customers, or gave them too much. The chocolate booth was already closed, as Mimi expected, its kerosene lanterns all snuffed out. The mudfish stall, whose rank odor engulfed the entire market, attracted dozens of customers clamoring to buy whatever they could afford of the day's catch. The pesticide seller was also open and doing brisk business. Mimi bought a small sack of pyrethrum for the bedbugs. Before getting into the line for lamb fries, her last possibility other than mudfish, she bought a tin of instant Postum, a jar of vitamins, a half-pound of lard and a liter of potato milk.

"The fries look small today," she said to the toothless meat cutter, who looked vitamin-starved.

"You don't want 'em, ma'am, then don't take 'em. There's lots of folks in line behind you."

"Give me eight then. And wrap them so they don't leak."

By the time her shopping was done, Mimi was exhausted. After just a few steps toward the market exit, she felt a sudden churning in her bowels. She feared she'd made her breakfast Postum without boiling the water long enough. Now she was on the verge of a bowel movement, but the open-air, public latrine behind the market was a horror to behold. She checked her money and there was enough to hire a jitney back to the cottage. Three or four cabbies stood around a kiosk at the end of the market's central lane, all dressed in black wool suits.

"Ride, ma'am?" This one had broad shoulders and his legs

were thick as hams. He would be a hard puller and a fast ride. The others were not as tall or well muscled.

"Yes."

"Where to?"

"Number 547. Out near the Mill."

"That'll be 10.46."

"Seems fair."

"Okay. Get in." Mimi set her packages inside the cab and sat in the well-worn seat.

"You ready?"

"Yes, hurry please."

The cabbie moved off at a lazy, loping pace.

That afternoon, at dusk, Jerry limped from the Mill to the cottage favoring his right foot. A painful red knob had appeared on the ball, just an itch at first, then a blister, and now, after a few weeks, a mound of miserable pain that had to be tended to.

He tried the back door. It was open. Mimi busily stirred potato milk into a pudding.

"You didn't lock the door, Mrs. Chung. I've told you to lock the door. The new neighbors look like trouble."

"I'll try to remember." They hugged. "Happy birthday, Mr. Chung. How's that poor foot?"

"It feels like I've got a rock in my boot."

"Go to the infirmary."

"The Doc's a quack. I'll come home without a foot."

"Be reasonable. It could be a tumor. Campers are getting them. The shoes they give us … something in the rubber soles … the glue, the solvent, something. Maybe the ground we walk on. I don't know."

"Yeah, I'm not the only guy limping around the Mill. I'll go see the Doc tomorrow."

"That's settled then," Mimi said. "The pudding's almost ready. It's Postum again. Chocolate is impossible to get anymore. Not even

carob. Forget cocoa. They never run out of Postum, thank goodness."

"What's for dinner?"

"Lamb fries."

"Were they out of mudfish?"

"There were flies on them. They smelled. Probably full of liver flukes, too."

Mimi brought a jar of water to the table. "Here, take your vitamins." She handed Jerry two green tablets. He swallowed one and followed it with a half-glass of the water, his lips puckering. "Water tastes pretty punky today."

"I boiled it a long time."

"It's making us sick. I throw up every morning."

"Why don't you talk to old man Ganzfeld? He runs the camp, he runs the Mill. He runs everything."

"Nobody talks to Ganzfeld. You listen, that's it. We think about organizing a union, but nobody's got the spirit for it. The last one that tried, Ganzfeld hit him in the head with a shovel. That's what I heard."

"Go wash, Mr. Chung. You smell like wet wool."

Jerry pumped rusty water into the sitz bath near the stove. "Any soap left?"

"Just that sliver. Soap seller at the market said a big shanty loaded with soap sank in the Canal. Suds for miles. People were bathing."

Jerry used a washcloth to wipe off as much of the sheep-stink as he could.

"Dry off, Mr. Chung. The fries are ready."

When Mimi served them, Jerry held one out at the end of his fork. "Ganzfeld says eating these makes us hard workers. We get the nuts, he gets the shanks." Jerry spit a chunk of lamb fry back onto his plate. "I'm sick of these. Next time get mudfish. I don't care how fresh they are."

"I'll try, Mr. Chung. That's all I can do. I'll get to the market as early as I can."

On his way to work the next morning, Jerry hobbled into the Chow Fun Diner, just outside the Mill's main gate, and took the only empty stool at the counter. "How about a cup of Postum and a griddle bun with lard, Mr. Fun?"

"You got it," Fun said, flinging a spoonful of lard onto the grill and placing a half-baked bun on top of it.

A fellow camper at a back table stared at Jerry, then came forward. "Excuse me, you're Jerry Chung, right? You work at the Mill."

"Mostly I shear. Sometimes I'm on the crank."

"I just started there last week. I'm Billy Ping. Hey, what's the story on that hole in Ganzfeld's face?"

"I hear lightning struck him when he was a kid and burned his nose off. The one he wears now he carved himself."

"I don't think I could live without a nose," Billy said. "I figure we've got noses for a good reason."

"You couldn't even smell a flower," Jerry said, dunking his griddle bun into the Postum and leaving an oily streak on its surface.

"Or shit," Billy said. "You'd be stepping in it all the time." He pointed to his own nose. "If I ever lose this, drown me in the Canal."

Jerry thought Billy's nose average and unremarkable as noses go, aside from the little blood blister at its tip.

"Yeah, me too."

On his lunch hour, Jerry hobbled to the Mill's infirmary, housed in an old shearing shed just beyond the little Mill cemetery. Workers new to the Mill were customarily told that the best and quickest way to the cemetery was through the infirmary, known for its unsanitary conditions and poor care.

When Jerry went into the waiting room, he sat on a hard bench and untied his boot string. Through a door crack, he could see Dr. Hammerstein in the washroom standing naked in a metal

tub and pouring water on himself from a jerry can. He was quite thin, almost skeletal, like most of the elderly in the camp. He saw Jerry looking at him. "What's your complaint, fella?"

"There's a lump on the bottom of –"

"That's a plantar wart. *Verucca plantaris*. It comes with your job." Hammerstein finished his ablutions and came out of the washroom wearing only a lab coat. "Let's have a good look at that thing." He sat on a wheeled stool and put on a jeweler's headset with a magnifying loupe. Placing his thumbs astride the mound of the wart, he pressed down suddenly and with force. Jerry cried out in pain.

"Sorry, there. Just diagnostic practice. Yes, this is a classic *verucca plantaris*, caused by a papilloma virus. All shearers get them sooner or later. See those little black dots on it?"

"I wondered about them."

"Commonly called 'wart seeds.' In reality they're small, clotted blood vessels."

"All day on my feet at the Mill. It's hard to take."

"They go away on their own eventually, but it could be years. You can dissolve the wart with a slightly acidic cream I make myself from willow bark." He held out a quart jar of the white cream." It'll take dozens of applications. And I warn you. Don't be surprised if other warts appear. They have a way of spreading."

"Thank you, sir."

"Apply the cream every night before bed and every morning when you get up. That will be 55.80, including the cream. It will be deducted from your pay."

The next day, Mimi received word that her once-removed cousin, Charlie Wang had been injured in a freakish accident on Monday and perhaps would not live. He had gone to the field to get a bale of hay for his sheep. When he removed the tin cover from the stack there was an explosion that knocked him to the ground. He landed

on his face, cutting his mouth and fracturing his skull. In addition, his iris was pierced and his septum was disengaged, all assuring him that, were he to survive, he would live the rest of his life in unending and unceasing discomfort.

"I'm going away for awhile, Mr. Chung," she told Jerry. "Cousin Charlie may die. He and I are the only ones of the family left in the camp. I might inherit something. He's got sheep, he's got acres, he's got money."

"I guess we can hope," Jerry said.

"I'm catching the overnight shanty. Please take care of things. Put out the pyrethrum, rub that cream on your wart every night. If I'm gone awhile, you may have to go to the market on your own. Or eat at Chow Fun's."

"Don't worry, Mrs. Chung. I won't forget anything."

Mimi packed a kitty bag that night and the next morning was gone before Jerry had awakened. She walked to Chow Fun's, hoping to find a jitney there. Two or three sturdy-looking cabbies stood outside, calling to pedestrians: "Hey, need a ride?" or "Climb on in, lady, you look tired," or "Lowest price in the Mill area, guaranteed." She gave 10 to one of them and said, "Can you take me to the Wang place?"

"Can do."

"Good. Wait here while I go in and get some breakfast." She handed him her kitty bag. "And keep an eye on this."

"Glad to."

She sat at the counter and ordered a slice of jelly cake and a cup of Postum. A woman sitting next to her wearing a knitted wool cap struck up a conversation. "I saw you hire a cabbie. Where are you off to?"

"My cousin's in a bad way. He had an accident. We've been estranged. I haven't seen him in years. But I feel obliged, you know, to visit him. He's way down in south camp."

"You're not going along Spillway Road I hope?"

"It's the only way, isn't it?"

The woman removed her cap. Her head was clean-shaven. "You must be very careful. There's a mad man out there. Look at me. Look what he's done. He appears clean and respectable, carries a little satchel like a doctor's bag with scissors, combs, a mirror, clippers, talcum, cream, a razor and a strop. They say he was driven insane by a lightning strike. And there you are with all that curly black hair. He'll drag you off, sure enough, and do this to you."

"I'll be in a jitney with a strong cabbie."

"Ha. So was I. He hit the cabbie with a truncheon and knocked him cold."

Chow Fun, listening to the conversation, approached. "Ma'am, he also jump a shanty captain, got a little shaky with his clippers and cut the man fairly bad. The docs stitch his scalp together right now."

"I don't have any choice," Mimi said. "I have to find out what my cousin left me, if he left me anything."

"Then here's wishing you all the luck," the woman said, lifting her mug of Postum.

Chow Fun shook his head. "You got good cabbie. I know him. He okay."

"There's a comfort," the woman said. "It's hard to get a good cabbie on that route. Some of them are just plain animals."

Mimi left 2 on the counter. Outside, her cabbie leaned against the building and stretched his legs. "You ready, lady?"

"Yes, but have you heard about this crazy barber out on Spillway Road?"

"You been talking to that bald woman in the hat. She tells everybody that story. It's a load of horse shit."

"That's a relief. My cousin is in poor condition. I'm in a hurry to get there."

"We're on the way, lady. Stick your foot out and give me a little kick in the hiney. It gets me going."

It was a pleasant feeling on the sole of Mimi's foot when it struck the cabbie's hard rump. After that she lay back relaxed as he made good progress for a few miles, keeping a steady, smooth pace. She was comfortable enough in the jitney cab that she was beginning to doze off when she heard a voice coming from a camphor grove. "I have a small caliber pistol in my pocket! Do what I say or someone will be killed!"

The cabbie stopped. The voice cried out, "You! The female. Get down and come with me." The voice was familiar. It had the same lack of nasality that Mr. Ganzfeld's had.

"I think it's more a plea than a threat," she told the cabbie.

"Should we run for it?" he asked.

"No, no. I'll go talk to him." She climbed down and walked slowly toward the camphor grove.

The voice swooned, "Oh, look at that rich, raven blanket of yours. I can't wait to give you a grooming. Go back and get your bag. You'll be staying overnight in a situation where coitus may take place."

Now she could see him, a stoop shouldered, pigeon-toed man of sixty or more years. A bandana tied behind his head covered his nose, face and mouth. He stood behind a rotting stump, the pistol held loosely in his hand, a black satchel lying at his feet. It was Mr. Ganzfeld himself. Mimi had seen him once or twice at the annual Mill pot luck and appreciation day. She had noticed something odd about his nose. It looked false, like balsa wood carved and sanded, perhaps held there by some kind of wheat paste glue.

"Just a minute," Mimi protested. "You know that's not lawful, Mr. Ganzfeld." She folded her arms. "I'm not going with you. I'm a married woman and you know it."

"All right, then." Ganzfeld raised the pistol and aimed it at the cabbie. "First, him. Then you." He held the pistol to his head. "Then me. Now, go and get your bag."

"No. I will not."

By this time, Mimi's cabbie had set down her kitty bag and

backed away from it, preparing to run.

"All right." A shot fired at the cabbie missed. He broke into a run, pulling his jitney wildly behind him. A second shot grazed his abdomen, yet he kept running. By the time Ganzfeld fired a third shot, there was no hope of hitting him.

Mimi was appalled that things had come to this. Goose flesh covered her in an instant. She pissed herself. She was cold, in shock.

"That oaf was no friend of yours. He ran like a deer," Ganzfeld said, taking off his nose and putting it in his pocket. "Now, I do have one strict and fast rule. This jagged hole where I once had a schnozzle … this is what a lightning strike can do. It must never be mentioned. I won't be wearing the false one. You'll simply get used to the way it looks, even when it drips."

"It isn't bad to look at. Just something missing, that's all."

"Good. We have that understanding."

Ganzfeld blew a wog of phlegm into the dirt before opening his satchel and taking out a comb. "I'm going to groom you some, then we'll go to the house."

She sat on the rotting stump as he combed her hair. "I'm putting more life into these black swirls," he said. "Did I tell you that I was once a very famous barber, before I opened the Mill and cornered the market in quality doll's hair and theatrical beards? I've coiffed Hollywood celebrities, ballerinas, presidents and tycoons." He took Mimi's hand in his. "You have damp palms, my dear. Don't be afraid. If anyone's going to get hurt here, it's going to be me." The comb's methodical movements through her hair, its gentle rake across her scalp, were like small doses of sleeping syrup. "Soon we'll go to the house," Ganzfeld said. "It's not very far. You'll bathe while I fix dinner. I think it will be braised lamb shanks with tomatoes, potatoes and carrots. I have a very nice garden. After dinner we'll discuss the pros and cons of coitus."

The combing came to a slow stop. Ganzfeld fished in his satchel behind Mimi's back and withdrew a paper envelope. In it was an analgesic of his own concoction. He tore open the envelope and

folded it in half. "Turn around, my dear. Let me see that handsome face of yours." When Mimi turned her head, he blew the powder into her face. "Breathe it in. It's just a relaxant."

On breathing it, Mimi felt removed from and above her surroundings, walking inches off the ground. It was probably traumatic shock, she decided, a reaction of the mind and body to the alarming events taking place, a kind of transference of disbelief into denial. She was now, for all intents and purposes, under Ganzfeld's control.

With no awareness of having gone any distance, though she knew they had, she and Ganzfeld arrived at a bungalow set atop a woody ridge of high ground. There was a putting green on one side, a flowing stream coursing through pine woods on the other. At the far edge of the property there were a dozen beehives. The garden looked well tended and productive. Eggplants, tomatoes, and bell peppers glimmered in the sun. The heads of sunflowers drooped with their weight of seeds. Young green melons sat atop mounds of rich, dark soil.

"We'll go in, you'll remove your clothes and I'll examine you before you bathe. The woods are full of ticks. They drop from the trees. The most patient beast in nature. A wood tick will wait years for someone to walk past."

The house was cool inside, even in the heat of August, well furnished and tidily kept.

"What am I to do now?" Mimi asked. "Am I being kidnapped?" She sat on a tufted velvet sofa and unlaced her boots. "Are you going to force me to have coitus?"

"Persuade, perhaps. But the choice will always be yours."

"They will come looking for me, won't they? The cabbie has friends at the diner. They'll come out to get me."

"I have friends at the diner, too. His friends are my friends, dear. And this is not a kidnapping. We are simply going to have a little time together here in the country. Isn't it pleasant and peaceful, far from the noise and stink of the Mill? This is my place of retreat. I

come here to think, to make plans."

Ganzfeld showed Mimi a room upstairs. It was not as well furnished as the others, just a mattress on the floor, a bag of golf clubs leaning against the wall, a vanity with a tray of grooming instruments and a closet supplied with women's clothing in various sizes. "You've got tweezers, a sharp razor, brushless cream, depilatory, beeswax, and a hand mirror. You'll be keeping yourself free of all body hair. I mean pubic and anal, too. Use the hand mirror and tweezers for that. Leave the head hair alone. Use that depilatory where you need it. Undress in here, then come down for your bath."

Ganzfeld made no attempt to touch her unclothed body as Mimi stood outside the bathroom for a tick inspection. "What will happen, Mr. Ganzfeld, if I don't do what you say?"

"I'll kill myself. Haven't I told you that already?"

"You did say that."

"All right. No ticks. Now, go bathe. You smell. And douche, too. There's a bag in there and some vinegar."

As Mimi douched, then bathed, Ganzfeld tied on a kitchen apron and began to prepare the shanks for braising. As she worked upstairs for more than an hour at removing her body hair, using every instrument and cream she'd been given, the shanks continued to braise until the meat fell from the bones.

Ganzfeld climbed halfway up the stairs. "Dinner's done, Honey Bun. I think I'll open a Spanish Rioja tonight. It will go well with lamb. And tomorrow I'll give you a mud pack. There's the most wonderful clay along the stream bank, full of nutrients and natural emoluments."

Mimi looked at her shaven body in the vanity mirror. She seemed more ghostly pale and thin than ever. Somewhere in her camp cottage, she recalled, was a photograph of her looking almost plump. That was before marrying Jerry and coming to the camp. Living on camp commodities, she'd shed weight prodigiously for awhile, five pounds a week, until Jerry took work at the Mill and

they were able to put a few more comestibles on the table.

She selected clean underwear, a Navy blouse, culottes and house slippers to wear for dinner. Beneath the clothes, her body hair gone, she felt every slight touch of the fabric against her scoured flesh.

Ganzfeld had set only one place at the table. "When I cook, I lose my appetite. If you can't smell, eating is just another dull habit," he explained, then stood behind her and combed her hair as she ate and drank. "I should tell you a little story, my dear. When I was a boy without a nose it was a terrible embarrassment. I had no friends. Although my family was well off, I suffered a genuine poverty of soul. I determined that eventually I would have the perfect nose, one that is indistinguishable from the real thing. I so long to smell a rose again." As he spoke, except as an accident of grooming, he avoided touching Mimi, and when he did, his hand recoiled as if stung by a bee.

Mimi said, "Excuse me for eating so fast. I haven't had any real meat in six months, or wine for years. You know it's not allowed in the camp."

"That kind of indulgence is not for everyone. But drink up now while the chance is there."

She poured herself a second glass. "I feel guilty. My cousin is injured, possibly dead."

"Death is death. What could you do to stop it?"

"Nothing, I suppose."

"You seem drawn and pale, maybe a little malnourished. There are those who say frequent coitus can do wonders for a woman's well being."

Mimi shrugged. "I'm very tired."

"You'll get your rest. There won't be coitus tonight. We have all the time in the world. I've dismissed my cook, my housekeeper, my gardener and even the retarded man who keeps the bees. We'll be alone and undisturbed for quite some time."

On the first night of Mimi's absence, the troublesome neighbors from cabin 545 showed a talent for opening locks. They entered the kitchen after Jerry had gone to bed and helped themselves, going about the business silently, not awaking him, even from his shallow sleep. But in the morning, when he went to breakfast, he found evidence of their rootings—the Postum jar overturned, the potato milk lapped up, gobs of lard scooped from the can and long, muddy boot prints on the plyboard floor. Worst of all, there were two bowel movements to clean up, one behind the pie safe, the second on Mimi's little round rug, as if a cat had left it. She had made the rug by stitching together a collection of old socks and worn out hankies. It would require a lot of soaking and scrubbing to get the stain and odor out.

The following night, Jerry remained vigilant, sitting up in the dark with his boots on. At about midnight, he heard the door latch being jimmied, then saw a long, narrow foot thrust through the door crack, followed by a dirty hand. Impulsively, he slammed his boot against the hand and foot until he heard bones crack and a sharp cry of pain.

"Ouch! You trying to break my foot you lousy son of a bitch?"

"Get out of my house!"

The hand and foot withdrew swiftly and a husky voice called out, "We're hungry, you scum sucker. Give us something."

A thrown rock bounced off the kitchen wall. A face looked in, contorted and stretched by the thin window glass. It was a girl of ten or twelve. "I'm starving, Mister. You got anything you can give me?"

There were footsteps on the roof. A desperate voice sounded down the stovepipe, "We can't find work. We can't find food. We're fucked. Help us out."

Jerry mustered a voice with both authority and menace in it. "Get on home! In one minute I'll come out there with my shears and cut you good."

At this, the neighbors backed away and shuffled off into the dark.

Jerry regretted using his warted foot to kick the door. Now he would spend the rest of the night sleepless and in pain. Before going to bed, he lathered the wart with acid cream and sprinkled pyrethrum around the bed to keep the bedbugs at bay. For a while he could hear the cream hissing and bubbling under the sheet, working on the scaly wart.

Two days later, the bad neighbor paid a more peaceful call. His knock was heavy and slow, as if he were throwing axes at the door. Jerry opened it a crack, bracing his foot against the bottom. Because the man was wearing a beekeeper's bonnet, his face was difficult to see. Twenty or thirty bees crawled on his coveralls. He said, "I'm setting up some hives behind my place and I'm telling all the neighbors not to fuck with them."

Jerry said, "No problem. We won't."

The neighbor lifted the bonnet's veil. Thick, black stubble covered a long, hanging jaw. His large yellow eyes looked like poached eggs. His tongue protruded unnaturally and was almost blue. "Sorry we had to bust in the other night. We were just plain hungry. I got two children and a dead wife. But things are looking better now."

"All right then. We'll forget all about it."

"Yeah, I guess we're even. You hurt my foot pretty bad. I got real long, sore dogs down there as you can see. Gotta make my own shoes."

Jerry looked down. "Yeah, I see. They're unusual."

"Well, all right, neighbor. You stay away from my hives, now."

"I promise."

"You know who I am?"

"No. Do you work at the Mill?"

"Used to, till my brother conked me good with a shovel one time for starting a union."

"You're Ganzfeld's brother?"

"He'd never admit it. He says I was born bad in every way. He don't have these feet that I do. His are tiny. I'm cursed."

"Sorry to hear that. Be seeing you around then?"

"I'll be around. I ain't finished yet."

On September 2nd, her birthday, Ganzfeld shaved Mimi's head, saying, "The last time I groomed you, I thought I saw a louse. It wouldn't be the first time a camper like you got an infestation."

Though no lice were found, Ganzfeld directed Mimi to shave her scalp daily and to rub it with mineral oil. "I love your look," he said, "So creamy white, and with a head that glistens."

Without hair, Mimi thought of herself as mannish and undesirable, and the underdrawers with holes in them only intensified the feeling. She entertained a momentary fantasy of Ganzfeld's delicate hands tearing them away.

Ganzfeld set aside the hot chutney to cool on the sideboard and put on his gardening togs. "I'm going to can some things before winter sets in."

Through the wide solarium window, Mimi watched him pinch caterpillars from the plants with a clothespin, then step on them. He picked a hamper of tomatoes, scattered compost over the entire garden, dusted selected plants with pyrethrum, watered, then came back into the kitchen. "Here's what the worms have left us," he sighed.

Lost in thought, Mimi marveled at the sudden twist her camp life had taken, and at her ease in adapting to it. There was a glimmer of concern for her cousin's welfare, but it was a very weak spark, and she soon began to live in the moment. "Shall I help you with the canning, Mr. Ganzfeld?"

"Yes, and call me Ganzy. Intimates do, and it's quite possible we'll be intimate before the day is over. I may decide to have coitus with you this afternoon. I want you to be clinically clean, though. Use plenty of depilatory, shave, tweeze, douche, the works. Then, perhaps you'll put on a nicer pair of drawers in front of me. I have a few silk ones other guests have left in a box under my bed. You'll

take them off in front of me and put them on again. Then you'll take them off again. These actions will be preliminary to coitus, if that occurs. Are you willing, or will I take you by force? I don't think you have any idea how manly I can be."

Not willing to risk Ganzfeld's temper, well known around the Mill, Mimi elected to go along and hope for the best. She worked most of the afternoon at cleaning and shaving herself, but afterward coitus was neither mentioned nor performed. Ganzfeld remained in his bedroom for two days before dragging himself out to move his bowels and heat up a can of broth. Before retreating to the bedroom again, he took vitamins and a tablespoon of honey.

When October came, and the cool autumn winds blew across the fields, Ganzfeld's hair had grown long and lay in dry, knotted strings on his shoulders. "It's over for me," he told Mimi one windy afternoon as he wept. "I'll never have a real nose. I'm going to shoot myself tonight. The decision is firm. Make no effort to stop me, please." He said he would be sitting in a tub of warm water when the deed was done. She was not to view the scene under any circumstances, but to make her way to the infirmary and alert Dr. Hammerstein.

To soothe him, Mimi combed his hair until dawn, at which time the weeping stopped and Ganzfeld elected not to die. When the pumpkins were deep orange and the air was crisp, he came back from the dark regions of the spirit to enjoy the chilly mornings in his garden, harvesting late season edibles like okra and cabbage.

During his long funk, Mimi's daily groomings had ceased, as had all mention of coitus. Her head and body hair were returning. She felt ever more assertive as the weeks flew by, and began to rehearse various escape scenarios. As things went, she wouldn't need them. Ganzfeld entered her room very early one morning. "Go where you like. Settle the estate. Go back to the camp and that dimwit husband. Our little idyll is over. Go now. Pack your bag

and leave right away."

"I should thank you for not … forcing … for not –"

"Self denial is a natural grace. Coitus digs the grave of the soul. Get out of here now. Go to your cousin's. Walk north one mile to the Canal. Catch a shanty there. You'll say nothing of this to anyone."

"Yes, sir … Ganzy I mean."

"No. We were never intimate. Don't call me that any longer."

"All right, then. I won't."

Mimi was packed and out of the house in less than an hour and ran all the way to the shanty dock, where she waited most of the day in the hot sun, swatting at gnats and mosquitoes, until a southbound shanty pulled in at dusk.

After a night long trip up the Canal, she caught a jitney at the mid-camp dock pulled by a lazy cabbie with bony shoulders and a high price of 30.12.

"That is steep. That is steep."

"Who has time to dicker? And look where we are. Five klicks from the Canal. It's a long way back. Who do you think carries old Charlie to the market when he needs some commodities? What does a cabbie have to do to get any attention, die and start stinking?"

"Here you are, then, 30 and 12."

"I'm glad that's settled. Now, please, put your foot against my back and give me a push."

For Mimi it was a great relief to be out of the confines of Ganzfeld's retreat, as comfortable as it was. She enjoyed seeing open spaces, fields of rye and timothy all the way to the horizon. Quite a few herdsmen like cousin Charlie and their families had come to this part of the camp for its rolling, treeless, grassy terrain. They'd brought breeding pairs of Cotswold sheep with them and eventually sold wool in quantity to the Ganzfeld Mill for the manufacture of doll's hair and theatrical beards.

Cousin Charles' cabin, Mimi thought, was unlike anything she'd seen back at the center of Mill camp. The first story was built

of common sense natural stone wall and the window stools were of cement. The second story was constructed with cement "logs" along the lines of an old wooden log cabin. In the front yard, the cousin had installed a cement bust of himself, whitened with zinc oxide.

Charlie Wang's nurse answered the door. "Hello. Who are you?"

"I'm Mimi. Charlie's my cousin, my second cousin. I've come to see him. I'm told he was injured badly."

"I'm sorry to say, miss, it was more than an injury. He is near death, but please come in. Someone put a little bomb in one of the haystacks a while ago. Probably vandals. There's been a plague of them lately. We think it was Ganzfeld's goons."

The nurse led Mimi through the cabin. The interior walls and molding were of natural wood. There were eleven rooms in addition to the bath in something of a labyrinthine arrangement. Chung's bedroom was at the very rear after many a narrow hallway and quite a few step-downs. It was dimly lit by a guttering candle and, to make things harder to see, half his face was covered with a quilt.

"Can he hear me, if I say something?"

"Who can tell? He's all but gone. If you had come sooner."

Mimi leaned over the bed. One of Chung's eyes was open, the other closed. His face seemed half dead, half alive. One of his cheeks was rosy, the other bloodless.

"Hello, Charles. This is Mimi, your cousin." The open eye blinked, half the mouth made an effort to smile.

"Can you say anything, Charles? Is there anything you have to say? What will happen to your property, your home? All your sheep? Is there a will?"

The nurse said, "He's left it all to the Mill."

Wang spoke something inaudibly. Mimi knelt beside the bed and placed her ear as close to his half-working mouth as she could. "What did you say?"

"He's demented," the nurse said. "Don't believe a thing. He's in

some other world."

Wang said, "You will find that all in creation is not real. Trust nothing."

"You see what I mean," the nurse said.

Though Mimi waited beside the bed quite a while, her cousin said no more. The eye and the mouth closed. Mimi thought this was the end. "He's passed on I think," she said.

"If not," the nurse said, "he will be soon. He's left money for cremation."

"I suppose there's nothing more to do," Mimi said. "The shanty doesn't leave until morning. May I spend the night?"

"Of course, you'll stay in my room. I'll be sitting up with Mr. Wang."

The nurse's room was cold, cramped, under a lean-to roof off the kitchen. The mattress was merely ticking stuffed with hay, the quilt tattered but clean. There was a lantern and a small dresser of splintered cottonwood and a chamber pot.

Mimi slept well enough. She awakened to find the nurse sitting at her feet. "He's passed on as I thought. We'll have a little ceremony tomorrow. Will you stay?"

"I suppose I should."

Jerry returned to work at the Mill on Monday morning. After two months of acid treatments, his wart had become dry, hard to the touch, and less painful. Now it was like a hazel nut rather than a rock in his boot. Fortunately, on Mondays, his feet could rest. He would be turning one of the big cranks with his hands and arms, which engaged a series of gears, capstans, pulleys and belts that operated the air-powered shearing tools.

Ganzfeld always assigned cranking duties at the last minute. Jerry never knew who would be at the crank next to him all day. Most of the men at the Mill were poorly educated "stoops," beset with pedestrian fears and trivial concerns. A lot of them worked

in the fields and barns with the sheep and weren't allowed on the shearing floor, or to run the machine that spun the wool into hair.

Today it was Billy Ping.

"How goes it, Mozit? Got you cranking today, eh?"

Jerry shrugged. "Doing one thing's the same as doing something else."

"How's that old wart?"

"I got it taken care of. It's shrinking. Not too much pain."

"Your wife back yet?"

"No. The cousin hasn't died, I guess, or gotten better."

"How long has she been gone?"

"A few months."

"Damn, that's a long time. You worried?"

"These things happen all the time. They pump them up with vitamins and they linger."

The two cranked without speaking until noon, when word came down the line that, as a special treat, Mr. Ganzfeld had set up a fish fry in the open air outside the Mill under the shade of an oak. When the noon bell rang, a salivating rush of workers hurried out. Chow Fun was chopping the mudfish into steaks with a cleaver as fast as he could, tossing them in flour and frying them in lard. The catsup was flying as the rowdy workers shoved and pushed for a position in line.

Ganzfeld said, "Don't be afraid, men. These fish are fresh from the Canal."

Jerry managed to get two mudfish steaks and a handful of soda crackers. But when he cut into the fish, a putrid odor rose up. "Shit. It's rotten."

Billy sniffed his. "That man can't smell a thing. I've got a bad one, too."

Jerry plowed his way to the head of the line and stood right in front of Mr. Ganzfeld. "Some of this fish is rotten, Mr. Ganzfeld. We'll be getting flukes."

"I tell him," Fun said. "He not listen."

"I netted them myself, early this morning. Why would I want to give flukes to my workers? There's a mountain of shearing to be done."

"You probably brought in a dead one or two. You need someone to smell them for you."

"I'm relying on Mr. Fun. Do any of them smell, Mr. Fun?"

Fun shrugged and continued chopping. "Bad head cold. Can't smell nothing."

Jerry volunteered. "I'll do it, Mr. Ganzfeld."

"There they are, in that metal tub."

Jerry sniffed every mudfish in the tub and threw the bad ones aside. Fun chopped the others into steaks

Mr. Ganzfeld patted Jerry on the head. "That's quite a smeller you've got, son. Your name?"

"Jerry Chung."

"Of course, Jerry Chung. Well, Jerry, best you eat lunch and get back to the crank. I'll call you if I need something smelled."

"Yes, sir. Be happy to."

Most of Monday was devoted to preparations for Charlie Chung's memorial service. There was food to be cooked and pastries to be made for a small circle of friends. The body had been taken away during the night and cremated. The urn with the cremains came back to the cabin in a jitney around midmorning. The nurse had arranged a place on the mantelpiece for it, flanked by a few candles and a photograph of her cousin posing with a pitchfork amid his flock.

With nothing to do after the mourners left, Mimi said goodbye to the nurse and, despite a chill in the air, hoofed it to the dock. There she got aboard an old shanty called the *Little Squirrel*, lit with kerosene lamps, jack-o-lanterns and flashpots placed here and there. Children played the game of Put-and-Take, by spinning a teetotum on the beaverboard deck and pretending to wager.

Through a window in the seating area just beneath the foc'sle, Mimi saw a ring of passengers sitting on benches, sipping Postum and chatting around a glowing pellet stove. She went inside to warm up. It would be an overnight sail up the Canal. The sleeping hammocks were on an unheated, outer deck and only a light blanket was provided. A bit of Postum would stiffen her constitution.

The last passenger to board before the shanty left the dock got his Postum and sat behind Mimi with a box of licorice drops and a bag of boiled peanuts. She could smell the licorice as the drops rattled around in his mouth. He tapped her on the shoulder. She turned.

"Peanut?"

"No, thank you."

"Hard to get, you know. These ones are boiled in salt water."

Mimi felt something bump the back of her clog. She looked down to see the point of the man's long, narrow foot. "'Scuse me, ma'am. I was born with these feet. Size twenty. Triple A. Always getting in the way…. Licorice?"

"Nothing, really. I don't want anything."

"How about a spoonful of honey. I got a whole jar of it."

"No!"

The *Little Squirrel* suddenly lurched, no doubt in the wake of a passing shanty, pitching passengers forward. The man behind Mimi took the opportunity to kiss the back of her neck, sucking at the flesh and biting her ever so slightly. This tried her patience and she stood up to scold him. "Touch me again and you'll get a taste of these." She made a fist and pointed to her knuckles.

"Now wait just a minute. I offer you some of whatever I got and what do I get? I get threats. What's a little smack on the neck? Where's the harm? My damn wife is dead."

Mimi held her breath for a moment. She drew a finger along her forearm and felt goose bumps. "I'm sorry. That's no excuse. Just keep to yourself."

The little sparring match ended just then as the Postum pot

was empty and the stove cool. Passengers were venturing out to the sleeping deck. Mimi located an empty hammock neighboring a rowdy family with a half dozen squirming children, but far from the oafish man with the long feet. It was also safely away from any chance of water splashing up from the Canal. The children eventually quieted and she was able to fall asleep, though she awakened after an hour or two and found the shanty listing to port dramatically. The absence of panic on board gave her the impression she was dreaming. After looking up to the foc'sle and seeing the calm demeanor of the crew, though they all stood at angles, her concern lessened and she went back to sleep.

The morning dawned dimly in a Canal fog as the *Little Squirrel* tied up at the south camp pier. Mimi climbed out of her droopy hammock to the *plip-plop* of mudfish feeding on scum. There was 10.35 left in her shoulder bag, just enough for jitney fare. She looked around for one, but other passengers had already hired all that were there. So she set out on foot, chilled and hungry, searching as she went for wild melon, ground cherry, mayhaw, anything edible. There were mushrooms everywhere, but she was afraid of them. Then, near a dead gum tree, she spotted the unmistakable whiteness of a puffball, one she knew to be safe. When she knelt to pull it from the ground, she saw another puffball a ways further into a stand of pines. Putting the first one into her bag, she went to the second one.

From that spot she could see a crude shelter made of bent-over saplings, crate wood and carpet scraps, its layered pine-needle roof missing in places. An orb weaver had stitched its web across the weedy opening. Mimi swept it to the side with a stick and crawled part way in. It took a moment in the gloom to see a man with bright red hair lying on the ground, and a few moments more to see that there was a small hole in his forehead, a pistol in his hand and blue flies roaming his face. A continuous trail of ants entered one nostril and left the other. He was wearing the typical dungarees worn by workers at the Mill. The name stamped above the pocket was Digby.

Called to Mr. Ganzfeld's office about midmorning on Tuesday, Jerry found him sitting at an oval desk wearing his balsa nose and trimming the hair on a doll's head. "Smell this, Chung. Smell the hair." He handed Jerry the doll's head. "We've been getting complaints."

"It does have an odor. Like laundry starch."

"Someone has been fucking my sheep. As every shepherd down the ages has learned, if you fuck them too much, the hair gets a stink. Who is it who's fucking my sheep? It's that new man, Billy Pong. You know him?"

"Ping. I see him around. We talk a little."

"Find out if he's the one. There's a bonus in it."

"I'll keep an eye on him."

"You find out who's been bestial with my wooly girls and I'll take you hunting at my country place. That's a promise."

"I'd really enjoy that, sir."

On leaving the office, Jerry noticed a black lambskin satchel sitting between two rosewood bookcases. It looked like a physician's medical bag. He'd been to the office several times before, but had never seen the bag. It was such an odd thing, he almost asked Mr. Ganzfeld about it, but changed his mind.

When he returned to the shearing line, Jerry saw Billy passing by, pushing a wheelbarrow piled high with sheep dung.

"Billy," Jerry whispered. "Stop a minute."

"How goes it, Mozit?"

"Fine, fine. Look, Ganzfeld thinks you've been dicking his wooly girls. Have you?"

"Who hasn't? If he thinks I'm the only one he's batty. Yeah, I tried it. I got kicked in the shins and she shat all down my boots. That was the last time."

"What am I supposed to tell Ganzfeld if he asks about you again?"

"Blame it on Digby. Big guy, red hair. Hasn't been to work in three weeks."

"I'll do that," Jerry said.

Mimi arrived back at the cottage an hour before Jerry got home from the Mill. She used the time to take a sitz bath with the last little bit of Epsom salts in the box. The little tub wasn't long enough for her to stretch her legs all the way, but sitting in the warm water with its salty feel on her skin was immediately relaxing. She lathered her close-cropped hair with fatted soap she'd taken from Ganzfeld's. The tub was close enough to the pellet stove that a kettle of water sat warming an arm's reach away for rinsing. Through the small window of the bathing area, she saw Jerry coming up the lane, still favoring his sore foot.

Before coming in, he shouldered a sack of pellets from the storage shed.

"Just in time," Mimi said. "The stove is almost empty."

"I'm so glad you're back. It's been months. How's your cousin?"

"He lingered on and on, but now he's dead."

"Your hair is shorter. Shouldn't be longer by now?"

"Cousin Charlie's nurse is very handy with scissors. She cut it for me."

"I see you have some new soap."

"Also from Charlie's."

"Did he leave us anything?"

"The sheep, the land, the house, everything he left to Ganzfeld, in payment of some sort of debt."

"It all goes to him eventually, why not now?"

"Have you gotten along well enough without me, Mr. Chung?"

"Same ole, same ole. The wart's a lot better. I put out plenty bug powder. The new neighbor broke in. Ganzfeld's brother. Says he is anyway. He's got brain damage. Ganzfeld hit him with a shovel for organizing a union."

"I hope you're not thinking along those lines, Mr. Chung."

"Nobody's organizing anything. He thinks we are. So we're blaming it on Digby, some guy hasn't been to work in a few weeks."

"Well, Mr. Chung, I know where this Digby is. I was going to tell you. I saw a body in a shelter on the way back. There was a hole in his head and a gun in his hand. His tag said Digby. You should report that right away."

"A red-haired guy?"

"Very red."

Mimi toweled off. "I brought home some puffballs for dinner." She put on fresh clothes while Jerry loaded the stove with pellets. He was thinking he might go ahead and tell Ganzfeld that Digby was the one fucking his girls. If it was Digby out there in the shelter, and it wasn't reported, he would be found soon enough anyway. Meanwhile, things could be blamed on him.

On Wednesday afternoon Mr. Ganzfeld called Jerry to his office.

"Well, who is it? Is it more than one man?"

"One man, sir. That's what everyone says. Name of Digby."

"Digby then. I'll give him a talking to he won't forget."

"Yes, sir. Anything else?"

Ganzfeld stood. "Yes. Fucking my sheep is one thing. Fucking me and my Mill, that's another thing. I have good reason to believe someone is making moves toward organizing a worker's union. Keep an eye on things, will you? Look for someone with a dull nature. It's the perfect façade. Behind it you'll find the steely underpinnings of a dedicated communard."

"I'll see what I can find out."

On the walk home, Jerry spotted Billy having a Postum at Chow Fun's and writing in a notebook with a pencil stub.

"Billy."

"Jerry. How goes it Mozit?"

"Good enough. What's up, anything?"

"Nah. You?"

"Ganzfeld thinks somebody's trying to organize a union. I told you what he did to his own brother."

"You know it's not me."

"Me either."

"Blame it on Digby."

There were dead gnats floating on the surface of Jerry's Postum. He scooped them out with a spoon. "Any idea what happened to him? What's the word around the Mill?"

"They say he got despondent when his mother died. They think he killed himself. Or maybe he jumped the fence and ran for it. Nobody knows."

"Okay. He'll be the organizer if Ganzfeld asks."

When Jerry got home he emptied his overall pockets onto the table. "Pay day today." There was 11 in bills and 36 in coin."

"Did you tell them about the dead worker I saw down the road? Somebody ought to go out there and get him. He was beginning to smell."

"I did. I did," Jerry lied. "It's taken care of. They'll send a search party." He dipped his finger into the lard can and licked it.

That summer, a raging, hot, clockwise wind blew undiminished over the camp for twenty-eight days, then died away with a frightening suddenness. It scoured the land of grasses, weeds and small shrubs and drove a big shanty boat into the Canal bank, where it sank into the muck.

Ten or twelve campers died in the storm, including a woman who was crushed in her cottage when the roof collapsed. A shepherd's wife also died. She had waded into the Canal for relief from the heat when the wind lifted her up over a hundred feet, then dropped her to the ground, snapping her neck.

Jerry and Billy talked about it over cups of Postum and griddle buns at Chow Fun's.

"It's like fucking manna," Billy said. "That boat was loaded. Me and the wife, we go out there and dig in the mud every weekend. I found some meat last Saturday. Sausages, chops, a bottle of beer, too. Can you believe that? The meat wasn't too fresh, but you boil bad meat an hour and its fine. I heard about some kid found a 21-pound ham. It was all shriveled and dusty. The kid bangs on it with his knuckle. It was hard as marble. I bet you could still eat it if you sawed through that crust."

"Me and the wife go digging sometimes," Jerry said. "I did find a bottle of some kind of cherry-flavored liquor. The label was gone. The wife says it's for a special occasion, as if we have special occasions."

"What's a special occasion? When they got chocolate at the market? I'd drink to that."

"Any news on Digby?"

"I heard they found a body in a shelter down toward the dock."

"Really."

"Half rotten. If it's him, who're we going to blame shit on?"

"Good point."

That afternoon, Jerry was again called to Mr. Ganzfeld's office.

"Chung. Have a seat. Have a seat. We need to talk. First of all, do you wonder about my youthful appearance? How old do you think I am?"

At first glance, other than its poor alignment and too-dark pigment, Ganzfeld's nose looked to Jerry like a real one. "I'd say about fifty, fifty-five?"

"Ha! Try again. I'll be seventy come Christmas. It's the new nose. It's made of pure Para rubber imported from India and stuck on with theatrical glue."

"It looks very natural."

"And another thing that keeps me youthful. I drink my Postum with a pinch of strychnine in it and I have never indulged in coitus. I take warm baths as often as possible. They have a splendid effect in toning the nervous system and quieting the tendency toward

undue generative desire. Tell me this, how often do you have coitus with Mrs. Chung?"

"Well, the camp regulations say no more than once a month."

"For good reason. Don't you see? We should avoid the stimulation and abnormal excitement of coital passion, which in the past and present has done so much harm in the lives of human beings everywhere. You should cut down or stop altogether."

"If that's the way it should be, M. Ganzfeld, then I'll certainly keep it to three or four times a year."

"Taper off, taper off."

"Is there anything else?"

"Any word on who's fucking the sheep?"

"We think it was Digby."

"Whose body was found this morning."

"I heard."

"So the fucking will stop?"

"I would think so."

"What about the organizing?"

"I'd bet it was Digby. That should stop, too."

"Good, good. That's a weight off my mind. Is there anything more we need to discuss, Mr. Chung?"

"Yes, sir. One thing. I looked into the camp well the other day. The stone lining's all caved in and there're tadpoles and minnows swimming in the water. That well needs some attention, sir. It's making people sick."

"I suggest you round up a gang of workers and get busy fixing it. Who wants to drink foul water? Anything else?"

"No, sir."

"All right, then, back to your shearing."

It was an icy cold day and snow was falling when Jerry and Billy attended Digby's internment in the company plot behind the Mill. A small headstone marked each of the graves and all were inscribed

with the departed's name, date of birth and death, and the maxim: *We Die That We May Die No More*. Diggers hacked away at the ground ice with picks, trying to finish Digby's excavation while the body lay uncoffined on a hay wagon, almost covered in snow. There were no relatives or family of his there, just a few shivering workers and Mr. Ganzfeld.

"How goes it, Mozit?" Billy's voice was hoarse.

"I'm still on my feet, man." Jerry pointed at the hay wagon. "Not like Digby."

"It's a real snot freezer today. Miserable."

"Good day for a funeral."

"I wish they'd hurry. He's frozen, but I can smell him."

"Can't get lime anymore," Jerry said, "Big shortage."

Billy pinched his nostrils closed. "Did that wife of yours ever come back?"

"She's back," Jerry said. "She had had a terrible time. Big delays with her cousin's death. He wouldn't go. It took forever."

When the grave was finally deep enough, Digby was lowered to the bottom with canvas straps. Ganzfeld, standing by, gave a brief eulogy. "When you sit with a nice girl for two hours, you think it's only a minute. But when you sit on a hot pellet stove for a minute, you think it's two hours. That's relativity. Digby's life was very short, but only in relation to eternity, which is very long. Thank you, men. Now, get back to work. Jerry, see me in my office."

Ganzfeld was not at his desk when Jerry arrived at the office. It was a chance to stand at the large, glass window and have a second story view of the shearing shed, the lambing barn, and Ganzfeld's thousand-head sheep herd feeding on winter rye. In full wool, they would soon need a spring shearing.

When Ganzfeld did make an appearance, he was carrying a half-gallon jar of honey and a shovel, which he leaned against a corner wall. "Sit down." He set the jar on his desk.

"Yes, sir. You wanted to see me?"

"I did indeed." Ganzfeld sat down and tapped the honey jar.

"You know what this is?"

"Honey?"

"Yes, it is. But more than that, it's the byproduct of …?"

"Bees."

"I'm looking for a better response. Try again. By what process is honey made?"

"I don't know. They suck it out of flowers, or it sticks to their legs or something."

"No, no. They suck nectar from flowers. Do you get my point yet?"

"No, sir."

"They store the nectar in a special stomach and take it back to the hive, where other bees suck it out of them and chew on it for awhile. This adds enzymes to the nectar, breaking complex sugars into simple, more digestible ones…. Are you with me so far?"

"I am, I think."

"So then they spread the nectar throughout the honeycombs and fan it with their wings. Water evaporates from it, making it into thicker syrup, which the bees eat. Now, what does all that add up to?"

Jerry shrugged. "They've got a pretty organized way to put food on the table."

"Exactly! The very word I was looking for. Organization."

Ganzfeld rolled his chair back from the desk, went to the corner, picked up the shovel and stood behind Jerry, who knew what was coming and clasped his hands at the back of his head to cushion the impact.

"You probably aren't familiar with that old expression, 'Where the bee sucks, there suck I'."

"No, sir."

"It was Shakespeare I believe."

"Yes, sir."

"Well, you and your organizing friends are sucking the life out of this Mill and there's nothing sweet about it."

"No, sir. I'm not organizing anything. You got the wrong guy."

Ganzfeld struck Jerry with the back of the shovel blade, breaking any number of small bones in his hands and knocking him to the floor.

"There, that'll teach you to fuck around in my hive with my workers."

Jerry looked at his crushed fingers and knew he would never shear again.

Once the snowstorm had passed, the weather gradually warmed. By the weekend it was quite comfortable out. Mimi hiked to the shanty wreck for an hour or two of scavenging. She brought two burlap sacks in case she found something worth hauling home and two sturdy oak sticks for moving rotted food around without touching it.

Scavenging nearby, were Ganzfeld's brother and his two children. He wore a beekeeper's bonnet and pulled a cart heaped with booty. His tall, stoop-shouldered son was eating a raw yam. The daughter sat on a pile of rags in the cart and sipped from a jar of clabber. "Hey, you," the brother said, pointing at Mimi. "I've seen you someplace or other."

"We're neighbors," Mimi said. "My husband says you people broke into our cabin and took food."

"Ma'am, we were starving. But now, thanks to this bountiful wreck, a dozen productive hives and whatever we catch in the Canal, we're getting by okay. I've got some yam tubers to plant, too, if my boy there don't eat them all."

The daughter climbed out of the cart and pointed to the horizon. "Isn't the sunset lovely?"

"It is," Mimi said, noting the girl's long, thin feet.

The brother ground the heel of his boot foot into the rocky soil. "Their mother lies dead and buried twice. She was in the cellar and that whole damn cottage fell in on her when the storm came

up. Poor woman had an unholy terror of wind. The first sign of a breeze she'd dash pell-mell down to the root cellar, throwing aside anybody in the way. Pushed the little girl down the stairs one time."

The son said to Mimi, "Here, have a licorice drop." He held out a palm full.

The daughter burbled and cried. "We wish we had our mother back."

The brother lifted her into the cart. "Come on, girl, let's get past all this hoopla and get on down the road. This is no place to be when the sun goes down."

Mimi poked around in the wreckage with her stick until moon shadows appeared, then made it back to the cottage with sacks only half full. In all she had harvested a small box of cornmeal, a serving spoon, a few candles, the tin of cookies, a bag of charcoal briquettes and an unopened box of toy soldiers.

To keep things going while Jerry's hands healed, Mimi went to work at the Mill, not as a shearer, but as a shed hand, who's job it was to throw the sheared fleece onto the wool table and inspect it for feces, skin fragments, twigs and leaves. If found, these contaminants would be tossed into a nearby barrel for later burning.

Just before lunch her first day, Ganzfeld made his rounds and stopped to talk to her.

"And how is Jerry doing with his hands? Will he be able to shear pretty soon?"

"Maybe in a few weeks. His grip is getting better. He plays with his toy soldiers. He picks them up and moves them around on the battlefield."

"Good, good. Any progress is good progress."

"May I say something, sir?"

"You may, of course."

"Jerry isn't guilty of organizing. He couldn't organize two rocks. You must believe that."

"It doesn't matter. What I'm trying to punish is the idea of organizing, not the organizer."

"Yes, sir," Mimi said.

"I do feel a bit guilty about this, so tell him I'll take him dove hunting at my country place." His tone grew more hushed. "You know how nice it can be out there, away from the camp."

"Yes, he'll be happy to hear that. When? What day?"

"I don't know. Whenever the season opens."

In addition to the painful cysts developing behind Jerry's ears that fall, he was having bad dreams, feelings of dread, tightness in the chest, numb fingertips, a slight fever, fiery, unrelenting heartburn, and a growing mass in the lower part of his throat.

He reported the symptoms to Mimi, who said, predictably, "Go to the infirmary."

"But the dreams," he said. "I'm lost in some city somewhere. I don't know anybody. I have no money, no papers. They talk in tongues or something. I can't understand what they're saying. The sun goes down. No streetlights. I'm scared to death. I feel bad all day after that."

"Bad dreams, bad health. That's what they say. You don't take your vitamins."

"They're just powder and salt. There's no vitamins in there."

"Then make an appointment with Hammerstein."

"I'm afraid of that place. Campers go in for hernias and come out cadavers. Bedbug bites get infected. Charts get switched, names get mixed up, the wrong medicines are given."

At four a.m. the following morning there was a knock at the cabin door. It was Ganzfeld with a waiting jitney. "Let's go, Chung. The doves are in the milo and the hunt is on."

Mimi helped Jerry button his fly and his shirt. His hands were not quite agile enough for that, or for tying his boots. In less than a half hour he was ready to go. Ganzfeld had been waiting in the

jitney, cleaning and oiling a shotgun, and was agitated. He told the cabbie, "If that dufus isn't out here in five minutes, we're going without him."

Jerry got into the jitney just as it was beginning to pull away. Ganzfeld said, "My share cropper has cut the milo and the doves are flocking in to feast. We'll bag a bundle."

"Thank you sir. I've never been hunting before."

"You'll have a gun, I'll have a gun, the dogs will flush them, then we'll shoot them out of the sky. When that's done, we'll eat them, my guests and I. A few years back, I built an in-ground pit a foot deep, three feet wide and six long, big enough to handle an eighty or ninety pound pig, twenty or thirty chickens and up to a hundred and fifty or so doves. I had the steel grill fabricated at a welding shop and the concrete bed poured professionally. The Canadian-made rotisserie alone cost over a thousand."

"This will be a real treat, sir. I'm looking forward to this."

"From year to year I do what I can to vary the way I prepare the birds. I've tried wrapping them in prosciutto, basting them with honey, rolling them in a spicy rosemary rub or stuffing them with sausage."

"Sounds great, Mr. Ganzfeld."

Before making a turn onto a two-rut road that led into the woods surrounding the milo field, the cabbie stopped at Ganzfeld's share cropper's cottage, a man called Possum. Ganzfeld said to Jerry, "I tried to keep a few beagles once, thinking this would save money. But the dogs barked incessantly and I ended up giving them to Possum, who now rents them back to me for five an hour per dog."

Jerry looked around and up into a wide bowl of clear sky. "I didn't think there was this much countryside anywhere around."

Possum spit tobacco juice into his palm, then rubbed it into his jeans. "Tell you what, Mr. Ganzfeld, I planted popcorn this year instead of milo. Smaller kernels. Doves love it. You'll do good out there. I guarantee it."

The claim proved true. The dogs scared up clouds of birds, so many that Jerry, despite his cramped fingers, joined Ganzfeld in simply firing birdshot into the cloud and bringing down two or three at a time. After four hours of this, their arms were so weak they couldn't hold up their guns. They had been too busy to count the birds, but Jerry said, "There's a hundred if there's one."

After getting the dogs into their cages, Mr Ganzfeld told the cabbie to take a walk. "Jerry and I want a little privacy. I'm going to show him how to field-dress the birds." The process, which Ganzfeld carried out amateurishly, spattered little bits of feather and gut into Jerry's face. After dressing, the featherless, headless doves were no bigger than baby chicks.

"We'll eat well tonight, my guests and I," Ganzfeld said. "It's too bad you can't stay. I said I would take you hunting. I took you hunting. The guests will all be close friends. No one from the camp will be there."

"All right, then. That's understandable."

"Good, good. We're even." Ganzfeld stuffed his hand in a pocket and fondled himself. "Get into the Jitney, Jerry. I'll sit next to you. We'll conclude this hunt like men do all over the world."

The two got into the jitney and Ganzfeld let his hand come to rest on Jerry's knee. "I'll do you first."

Jerry shrugged. "Do what?"

Ganzfeld produced a jar of petroleum jelly from beneath the seat. "After I do you, you can do me." He undid the fly of Jerry's khakis button by button and handled him until he was erect, then massaged the tip with his forefinger. "Wow," Jerry sighed.

Ganzfeld curled his hand around Jerry's hard member and moved it slowly down the shaft, then up again, until Jerry's head lolled back. "God, this is so good. Here I go." When he came, Ganzfeld caught the discharge in a bandana and held it beneath his false nose. He said, "I only wish I could smell this. Do *me* now."

Jerry focused his attention on his left hand, then his right, and wondered if he could form a cup or even grasp with either of them.

"My hands aren't completely healed yet, Mr. Ganzfeld. Look." He held them out, flexing the fingers as much as he could.

Ganzfeld looked quickly at the swollen knuckles and out of place joints, then turned away. "Oh, well, Jerry. I guess I had it coming. I tell you what, it's time for me to get back and cook these birds. The guests will start arriving at seven. Right now my cook is probably dumping hickory chips into a bucket and wetting them down with the hose. He will then spread charcoal in the brick-lined pit, set out chairs and wipe the summer's dust from them. He'll get the dandelion fork from the garage and uproot every one he can find. This is all part of the get-ready for the dove fest. I've finally decided. I'm going to stuff them with liver of unborn lamb this year."

"I really appreciated the hunt, Mr. Ganzfeld."

"I felt a little guilty. I thought I owed you something. After all, I made an example of you to teach the other workers another lesson about organizing. I didn't know whether you were a union man or not. I picked your name from a list of shearers and I regret the damaged hands. Frankly, I doubt you'll ever shear again from the looks of them."

"Thank you, sir. Things go the way they go. If I can't shear, I'll find something else to do."

"Mr. Fun's always looking for kitchen help down at the diner. I'll put in a good word there for you."

"Thanks again, sir."

"I'd give you a few doves to take home, but they'd spoil without ice and what little I've got, I need. I'll have my driver take you back to the camp."

"All right, sir."

Mimi left a note for Jerry: *Gone to the night market.* She walked first to Chow Fun's to get a jitney. It was dark by the time she got there and no cabbies were around. She went in to wait for a jitney and

have a Postum.

"We got real coffee tonight," Fun said. "You want a cup? It won't last long, believe me."

"No, thank you. I don't like stimulants. Postum's a lot healthier. It's got wheat bran, molasses, corn syrup, all that good stuff."

"They tell me there's not much of a wheat crop this year. Better stock up on your Postum. Somebody's been sinking the big shanties that come up from way, way south."

"Where's all the cabbies? There's always one or two out there all the time. I wanted to be at the night market when it opened."

"A new one working market route tonight. Very slow. Name of Billy. He show up in a little while." Fun glanced up from the rag he was wiping with. "He there now."

"Billy Ping?"

"Say he work at the Mill. He got a jitney. He moonlights."

Mimi sipped her Postum until the cup was dry, then went outside. Billy sat in his jitney looking at his hands. He was jaundiced. Even the whites of his eyes were as yellow as egg yolks.

"Hi, there. You're the Billy Jerry talks about, from the Mill?"

"Yeah. I know Jerry."

"I'm his wife."

"Oh, yeah…. Please, don't let word get around the Mill I'm pulling a jitney. It's a big no-no with Ganzfeld. If you work at the Mill, that's it. No other jobs allowed. You saw what he did to Jerry. Where to?"

"The night market."

Billy got out of the jitney and Mimi got in. "I want to get to the market before they run out of everything."

"We're on the way." Billy secured the last buckle on his harness. "Give me a hard kick. I'm weak. I've been sick. Hammerstein says I got liver flukes from mudfish."

"Jerry isn't very well either, and my digestion is iffy iffy. We think it's the water."

"Yeah, it's stupid. The water you take your vitamins with

makes you sick."

Mimi leaned back and twice slammed the heel of her clog into the small of Billy's back. "Ouch! Ohhh…. That was good. We're off."

It was a two or three mile ride to the market. By the time Billy had pulled the jitney there, he was feeling faint. "Go get what you need. I'll be napping in the jitney." He waved to her as she joined the surprisingly small crowd of shoppers, so small that many of the kiosks, pavilions, stands and booths had no lines at all.

She saw a lantern hanging above a sign that said FRESH MUDFISH—NO FLUKES. "Big week for muds, ma'am," said the counterman. "Cheap as dirt and pretty fresh. I'm letting them go at 5 an ounce." The fish were stacked in crates, attracting flies, which the counterman shooed with a twirling towel. "Two for 7. Guaranteed near fresh."

"Give me two. No flukes, you say?"

"No flukes. But cook 'em good to make sure."

"I will."

The counterman wrapped the mudfish with newsprint. "Not many people shoppin' tonight, ma'am. I thought I'd be sold out by now. I hear there's a sickness going around."

"Almost everyone in the camp's got something or other."

Mimi moved on to a booth selling johnny cakes and honey. She bought six cakes wrapped in wax paper and put them on top of the meat. Then it was a stop at the pesticide booth for more pyrethrum and another at the produce pavilion for whatever was available. Today it was carrots, a bit shriveled and fibrous, and cabbages no larger than Mimi's fist. She could boil them with the meat, thicken it with potato milk, and make a passable stew. She considered the possibility that Jerry would bring home some game, but didn't want to count on it.

Neither Billy nor his jitney could be found when Mimi was ready to leave the market. She asked a cabbie if he'd seen him. "Yeah, yeah. I did. Some fellow came up and they were talking

awhile. It looked like old Doc Hammerstein. He got into Ping's jitney and they took off. You want a ride somewhere? Where to?"

"Out near the Mill."

"Here, get in. I'll take you."

That evening, after letting the mudfish stew with the cabbage and carrots for hours, Mimi served it to Jerry. When it had cooled a little, he spooned some into his mouth. "I must have shot fifty doves. Did he give me any? Even one?"

"Your friend Billy is pulling a jitney at night. He took me to the market."

"What an idiot. Ganzfeld'll kill him."

"He's got liver flukes. He's turning yellow."

"He probably doesn't cook his mudfish enough."

"I asked him to wait for me while I shopped, but when I was ready to go he was gone. Another cabbie saw someone shake his finger in Billy's face, then get into his jitney and off they went. He thought it was Ganzfeld."

A week later, on Monday, preparations for shearing were underway. Shears were being sharpened at a grinding wheel, the edges then finished with fine-grit sandpaper. The crank mechanism had been taken completely apart, cleaned and oiled, then put back together. Some of the men were rounding up sheep from the far corners of the Mill's thousand acres. Ganzfeld stood on a catwalk above the shearing floor overseeing the activities.

Mimi, having noticed Billy's two-week absence, stayed busy in the shearing shed, sweeping small piles of wool into larger ones, looking mostly at the floor. She feared the worst for him.

Ganzfeld's voice echoed through the shed. "You. Mimi. Come up to my office."

Mimi chilled. Her knees lost all sensation as she went up the stairs. Each foot had to be consciously lifted, then set down on the next step. She'd never been called to the office before and worried

about what awaited her.

She knocked on the rough wooden door. It was Ganzfeld who answered and let her in, then sat on a chair near his desk.

"Why do you want to see me? Have I done something wrong?"

Ganzfeld squirmed and rocked the chair side to side. "Your husband, he was a friend of Billy's, wasn't he?"

"He knew Billy."

"I'm sorry to tell you, but Billy was found dead this morning, floating in the Canal, still harnessed to the jitney. They say he was in the water quite some time, as long as a week. Not much left of him. He shouldn't have been moonlighting. I discourage it."

"Billy gave me a ride to the market last week."

"In complete defiance of a cardinal rule at the Mill, no second jobs."

"Is that all, sir?"

"No, as a matter of fact, I wanted to extend an invitation. Tonight, at Chow Fun's, it's all-you-can-eat *lo mein*. I arranged delivery of all the ingredients, including the noodles. Very hard to get, you know. Go down and spread the word. By all means, bring Jerry along."

Jerry and Mimi arrived at Chow Fun's a full hour before the special was to be served and had their pick of booths.

"You way early," Fun said. "We still getting ready. You want Postum?"

"Yes," Jerry said, "two mugs."

"With vitamin?"

"Please, yes," Mimi said. "We don't feel too energetic."

"OK, two and two."

Though the kitchen area was obscured by a bamboo curtain, there was someone back there working over steaming pots.

"Mr. Fun, You've got help tonight," Mimi said.

"He good worker. One problem. He always stepping on my

feet." Fun thought this very humorous and laughed all the way back to the kitchen.

When he parted the curtain to go in, Mimi said, "That's the neighbor in there. Jerry, go ask him if he knows what happened to Billy."

"Too bad about Billy, but we don't need to get involved. Let's mind our own business."

"They found your friend in the Canal. You should care."

Jerry held out his gnarled hands. "What good would caring do? He wasn't a friend. He was a fellow worker. We were on the crank together a few times."

Fun brought the Postum and vitamins. "My helper say he know you."

"We're neighbors," Mimi said.

"Sad man. Wife dead. Two stupid children. He got it hard."

As the *lo mein* serving time approached, Chow Fun's filled with Mill workers and their wives. There was talk that Ganzfeld would come by for a bowl himself.

"They say the boss come about eight," Fun announced, standing on the counter.

The *lo mein* was ladled into mismatched bowls in the kitchen and Mr. Fun then brought them out, as many as ten or twelve on a round platter carried above his head, balanced with one hand while the other held a bunch of chopsticks. When he came to Mimi and Jerry, he lowered the tray so that they could reach their bowls of *lo mein*. "Helper say to tell you, better days ahead."

"I hope so," Mimi said.

"I doubt it," Jerry said.

Fun shrugged and moved on with his tray.

Ganzfeld's jitney stopped in front of Fun's. Someone saw his driver helping him out of the seat. "He's coming. He's coming," they shouted. The chatter subsided. Eating stopped. When he entered, Fun went to the door to greet him. "Come in, boss. People having good time."

"Yeah. Thanks for this great meal, Mr. Ganzfeld," one of the workers said.

Others raised their mugs of Postum.

Ganzfeld's driver helped him to stand on one of the metal tables. It was noticeable to everyone that, aside from the prominent blood blister at its tip, his nose looked perfectly natural, as if he'd been born with it.

Fun offered Ganzfeld a mug of Postum. He sniffed it, then declined. "I'll just talk to my workers and then go." He cleared his throat. "As you all know, the Mill is the lifeblood of the camp. We all depend on it. But when hard times come along, where's the market for Santa beards and doll's hair? Where are all the stage productions that require wigs and beards? What kid cares about Santa any more? How many little girls play with dolls? What I'm saying is, I'm closing the Mill tomorrow. I'll give you a month to pack up and move on before we demolish the cottages. But the news isn't all dark. The sap is exultant in the trees and spring is just around the corner. The turpentine camps will be hiring."

Before the workers had absorbed the dispiriting news, a cleaver flung from the kitchen struck Ganzfeld in his upper back. He fell forward off the table and was caught by his driver, who lay him gently on the floor, face down. The cleaver had penetrated four or five inches. Though his legs moved and his fingers twitched, it looked to anyone close by to be a paralyzing if not a mortal wound.

"It was the neighbor," Mimi said, "his brother. I saw him throw it."

The neighbor came out of the kitchen through the bamboo curtain, loosening the straps of his apron. No one made a move to accost him. He seemed quite calm and purposeful as he went to Ganzfeld and stood over him. The driver backed away as the neighbor pulled the cleaver free, then turned Ganzfeld over with his long foot and said, "Glory be, brother. That's all for you."

A few patrons, including Jerry, stood up to get a better view. "I know that nose," he said. "That's Billy's nose."

In just two days, graves had been dug for both Billy and Mr. Ganzfeld. The services, such as they were, were held at the same time. Chow Fun was there. Jerry, Mimi, and a few Mill workers had come to see Billy off. Most had stayed home that day. The guilty neighbor, in custody, was tied to a hackberry tree just over the cemetery fence with a grain sack over his head and shoulders. What little light came through the weave would be the last he saw. Later that afternoon, he would hang from the branch just above him.

With Ganzfeld dead, the Mill lacked anyone prepared to preside at burials. The nearest thing to it was Dr. Hammerstein, who was urged into service to say a few words over Ganzfeld. "He was a good man, on balance, overall, when all is said and done, Ganzy was. I hope he has a good time in Heaven, with a factory to run or something like that. At least he's going with a nice good nose, one that I put on him. I think we can count on the fact that Heaven smells pretty good. Well, I've said enough. May he rest in peace."

Billy's body had been hastily readied for burial. Someone had stuffed a coiled handkerchief into the hole left by his cleanly excised nose. He would be interred without anyone "official" speaking over him, although Jerry did step forward to say, "Tough luck, Billy boy." Mimi cried a little, not so much for Billy, or the doomed neighbor, but at the thought of the Mill closing down, and the night market soon after. Where would they go? What would they eat? As grim as life in the camp had been, could they find anything better?

Chow Fun, who campers thought of as reasonably wise, said to as many as could hear him, "Chow Fun move to turpentine camp. Turpentine a new thing. Everybody want it. Burn for fuel. Good cough syrup. Camp not far. Up Canal, thirty, forty mile. Plenty jobs. Open up restaurant again. Everybody smart to go there."

"I'm going," Hammerstein said.

Most of those who'd come to the services stayed behind to

watch the execution. Hammerstein paid three of the workers to take care of hanging Ganzfeld's killer. They were clumsy in doing it, and the poor man dangled for hours with one toe able to touch the ground. Most of those attending were put on edge by the cruel spectacle and left the cemetery grounds before it was over.

Jerry and Mimi spent another two weeks at the cabin. On their last night, when the market shut down tight for the last time, they were not alone in going down to the wrecked shanty at low tide to dig for something to take along to eat on the road to the turpentine camp. Despite the crowd, Mimi managed to crawl under a vitamin-starved scrum of hungry campers and come out with a tin of salted mudfish. When they got back to the cottage, Mimi took down the bottle of cherry-flavored liquor they'd salvaged long ago and proposed a toast to their coming relocation.

"At last, a special occasion," she said.

"Special or not," Jerry said.

They drank from the bottle until it was gone.

Though the following day dawned with a cool drizzle, a grey sky and headaches from the liquor, Jerry and Mimi packed a few boxes and several travel bags then waited at the roadside for a jitney to take them to the shanty dock. Grasping the handle of his travel bag was encouraging for Jerry, whose hands were finally mended. "We could have stayed another month or two," he said. "You could have gathered greens and I could have caught mudfish."

"I don't think so, Mr. Chung. The market is closed. Chow Fun's is closed. Everyone's going to the turpentine camp."

Mimi looked up and down the lane, hoping a jitney would come into view. Instead, it was a cart loaded with household possessions and jars of honey. Atop the pile sat a young girl crying.

"It's the neighbor's children," Jerry said.

As the tall son pushed the cart past, he recognized the Chungs and stopped. "We're taking this honey to the new camp."

"We're very sorry about what happened," Mimi said.

"She saw him hanging. She watched them cut him down," the

son said. "She won't stop bawling."

"I'm going to cry for the rest of my life," the girl sobbed.

"Poor Billy, too," Mimi said. "We knew him a little."

"Well," the son said, "I've got a long haul ahead of me. I better get on down the road. No time for any more hoopla."

The girl stopped crying for a moment. "I heard we'll get showers and clean clothes when we check in."

"That would be nice," Mimi said. "We'll see you there."

"Save us a jar of that honey," Jerry said.

In the hours the Chungs spent waiting for an empty jitney, they saw hundreds on the move by foot, some hobbled with plantar warts. One of them paused to warn that all the shanty boats and jitneys were full and the only way was to walk and to start soon. Rumors were spreading that only a few dozen, maybe a hundred would be hired on at the turpentine camp and the rest would have to move on. There would be other opportunities it was thought. Work camps were always hiring. Word had it that a brand new cough medicine factory was opening about fifty miles north. A passerby said, "Hell, my brother just told me they need fifty or sixty pill makers down at the vitamin plant. You folks better get going."

Mimi looked over her travel bags and selected one of the three to take with her. There would be no way to carry them all. She looked at Jerry with weary eyes. "Eventually, Mr Chung, why not now?"

Jerry slung a bag over his shoulder and the two went into the road to join the flow of hopeful workers.